The Great Quill

The Great Quill

by Paul Garson

DOUBLEDAY & COMPANY, INC.

GARDEN CITY, NEW YORK

1973

The following was not written under the influence
of any stimulant or depressant; it was written
when the walls supporting the doors of perception
were removed. The Mind is the Book of all books.

First Edition

ISBN: 0-385-04910-2
Library of Congress Catalog Card Number 73–80014
Copyright © 1973 by Paul Garson
All Rights Reserved
Printed in the United States of America

To all who ride through nightmares
taking notes

In the beginning of the Second Time,
when all else save the Two Isles
had fallen beneath the thirsty waters,
there arose a mighty race and among them
One who wore a face of Flesh, the great
Quill

The Great Quill

Twenty-five hundred years ago, long before the World Holocaust had devastated the Earth, Shakespeare had sipped ale in this noisy tavern. But it made no difference to Francis, the brew was bitter to his lips.

Beating his breast had left too many bruises; self-flagellation was too helter-skelter, bead swallowing made waste, and he himself thought the smell of gangrene would let the wolves out. Amid the laughter and carousing, he finished his joke, buttoned his trousers, and left the tavern for a walk in the gardens across Cambridge Street, looking left and right for any sign of the bailiff's men. Horsebackers came dislodged from the night and boldly clattered across the cobblestones toward Westminster Bridge's blackened remains.

Monkeyshines, he thought, these young toughs and their flying heels in the face of gentlemen and their ladies out for a promenade. He had to get the package delivered in the morning or his life was not worth a bee's fart and he knew it. Life at any risk was not worth the scalpel or the jig-saw wrench of the rack. He shivered at the thought of the Baron's dungeons. But he had made his choice, his decision, and would not go back on his word or his fright.

The lesion on his left hand festered; he thought he could take his payment and summer in Lourdes for the cure. The wound had never rightly healed; certainly the leeching had not helped. He wound the soiled linen napkin around his hand, bracing his eyes to the cold draughts of wind blowing from the north. Those damned quill, he thought as he neared the scarred ruins of Parliament.

Bringing himself to the knees of realization, he charged the gateman to let him enter.

"And who are you that I should let you pass?" asked the burly rag-stuffed guard.

"Francis of North Dunnetowne."

"Yes, my Lord. I'll unbar the gate. I'm sorry, I didn't recognize your mask."

As he entered the thick shrubbery the vegetation took on spectral forms in the dim dinginess of the London twilight; wraiths and ghouls bedecked with tomb-swept flowers bent and unbent and blew themselves into puffs of fog and clouds of shadow. He was to meet his man Greensby at the trellis of rhododendron in the southwest corner of the botanical gardens. Greensby had let himself in during the day with the regular visitors and had remained hidden when the grounds were cleared for the night. Big Ben knelled the dark hour beyond the bomb crater.

Turbulence in the upper atmosphere caught his attention; he looked through the long sickle-leaved branches at the conjunction of Mars with the moon's pitted limb. Bath and Sutton Downs and the cough of the high-hipped whore at Distall's House turned his head southerly to the appointed rendezvous. He noticed saplings and the spurs of cedar tendrils lacing the iron grating over the bench. He took his time about undoing the rainwear over his boots, feeling for the hilt of the Saracen dagger secreted there. He would have liked to be in the thigh-thick embrace of the red-haired harlot, or drinking his yard, or anything besides thickening the hair on his hand with the blood of a man only as evil and frightened as himself.

He took a deep breath and made his way to the stand of Chinese bamboo. In among the tall fibers the silhouette of a man shunted back and forth; in the darkness he could make out a curious moaning sound coming from the wind and bamboo. He stuck his arms into his legs and spread back the curtain. In among the creaking sounds of wood the man Greensby stood tattered as a Norse hare.

Someone had done the dirty work for him by the look of surprise in Greensby's still-opened eyes. The bamboo was so closely compacted that the corpse had had no room to fall. It dangled like a Chinese lantern, all thin papery and gaping. Quickly, Francis switched on his killing mask, sensing danger.

The ancient dagger had become aware in his hand and took Francis' hand high into the air, whipping his body around to meet the onrushing attack. The dagger reared back to strike and took the hand holding it along. Hardly a pip-squeak of a sound came out of the man when the knife threw his throat into a disgorged gurgle. The man's face died above his throat with a look of remnants as if it said, "I thought it was so that I would be the killer this time," as if surprised; "I thought it was so, perhaps it was a wind leaf." And it died, his face, and he died, and the killing knife sang on between the frozen fingers. "I kill, I kill, I kill, I kill, I kill. You kill, he kills, we kill, you kill, they kill." It sang the song of a refrain of happy madness, glory blood drowned deathness as it sank into the neck again and again; And it sang, "I kill, you kill, he kills."

The body was dead many times over before Francis was able to wrest the knife away from its frenzied stabbing. The mutilated body lay in a glistening puddle, its legs rubbery and tangled among its arms.

Francis stood back from the gore, his head reeling. The dagger still vibrated in his hand, sprang forward in quick spurts in its attempt to get at the throat again. With all his strength Francis restrained it until he was able to secure the knife into the boot scabbard where it shook and whispered, "I kill, you kill, he kills," until Francis had long left the park and the burnt-out city, to look over the devastated countryside.

Cynically to himself he said, "And they called it long ago, *Great* Britain."

Q

He found no papers or paraphernalia of any interest on either of them; certainly no sign of the consumptive Harlequain. Lest he fall prey to the wary patrol, he quickly stilted the bodies deeper into the embrace of the stand of bamboo, briefly pausing for a slight shudder of envy and cold. He left the garden in sight of the Baron's black pinnacle rising out of the center of the town like Satan's horn. He made straightaway for the Piltdown Inn and a cup of brew with his friends Snile and Frath, two journeymen of his long acquaintance, but they were not to be found. The others quaffing their ale made no bones about their feelings; Francis was well known to be in the employ of the Baron. He was left alone at the large table pitted with curses and oaths. A pewter mug and a swollen hand made the humble table bleaker, more desolate in his eyes. He knew no good would come of his alliance with the Baron; he had awakened in his straw pallet with a palsy-quaking cheek and a feeling of deep despair. Suicide, the forbidden thought, had been the first thought he had upon waking in the new day. "Suicide," the forbidden word, he said to himself, as he downed the last dregs of his cup.

He had seen nothing but dead men this past fortnight. He himself would have been hoisted among the cherry trees for the play of the sharp-beaked crows had he not sworn allegiance to the Baron and signed his name to the registry of agents years ago. Agent provocateur, the Baron had said. "Assassin," whispered Francis.

He had the men, Francis among them, lined up in rows of a baker's dozen in the inner hall of the dark fortress. He could see the citadel now, hovering on the hill over the city like a mailed fist, ready to crush anything that moved under its iron shadow.

The Baron had smelled of scorched earth and shrapnel when he had reviewed the newly acquired agents, recruited from the prisons and jails of the surrounding townships and stagnant villages.

The Citadel it was called, and the thugs of love often called it the home of all pain where honest men became cinders and a girl's life meant stale cheese. Little had he known the outcome of his paltry crime would have levered him into the gullet of no recourse but to do as the Baron ordered or die beyond recognition.

Holy spires loomed jagged in the cold moonlight as if all the churches in the world had broken their steeples in anguish over the rule of terror and chaos that pervaded the lands of the earth.

Whole cities of common people burned themselves with quick-
lime rather than eat the marrow of their fellow men as the Baron
had commanded. Their teeth on edge until the end of time and
their children's children unreclaimed garbage in the heap of
civilization's lesser antiquities. "In the year of our Lord," muttered Francis, "four thousand years A.D.—After Death."

The Baron had stood in his chromium battle armor, fully seven
feet in height and as broad as a Chesteron ox, his face cut enor-
mously evil with the eyes of a hell hound; his teeth clacked when
he spoke beneath the shining gleam of his vizor. He carried a
heavy baton carved and fluted with elephants and dragons. His
boots rang like cannon shots through the corridors of the fortress
as he paced through the ranks of men. "Francis of North
Dunnetowne," he called out in that curiously soft voice, echoing
from beneath his mighty headgear. "Francis of North
Dunnetowne. Take this infidel's dagger that I took from the
throat of a Moslem dog I slew in Jerusalem and find the heart of
my enemies."

"Who are your enemies; how will I know?" Francis had asked.

"The dagger knows; it will find its mark; you merely are the
vehicle of its approach. Carry it with you wherever you go and
obey its command, else lay your own life at stake. Do as I command and your life shall be enrichened by all the pleasures heavy
drops of gold can buy."

The imagery of his induction slothed away on three toes into
the frays of his memory. He walked the streets in the gloomy
light of his own drowned soul. Shrunken and covered with
seaweed, it lay broken shouldered and limp within his body. His
hand throbbed. The cold air drew the pain out in sharp spasms.
His breath was like splintered glass in his chest. If he could only
get to Lourdes and the miracles. The hermit had told him to go,
but his only chance for redemption lay in a visit to the holy
shrine. But it lay across the channel, as far away to him as the
hopes and dreams he had as a child among the flowers and
heather of the hill country. As far away as Innisfree. Innisfree,
the *Other* Isle.

The town lay swarded in the consequences of its prostration

to the Baron; blackened and notched for easy identification, it lay huddled and beaten. Every now and then small sounds of anger and frustration would crack the utter silence until Agents of the Baron brought their whips and strangling wire.

It was the red-haired whore he sought out. "She's in the rest area," said the guard at the desk. "She has a fifteen-minute break." Francis showed him his identity papers and was ushered to the back room where Rochalle rested on her elbows at the small table in the center of the dark room. Her hair curled between her fingers, she looked up when he entered.

"You?"

"I came to see how you were."

"Can't you see"—she began to cough violently—"that I'm very well."

"I may have enough to buy our way free of here soon."

"No one has that much money."

"I'll have enough, by tomorrow morning."

She wiped her mouth free of clinging hair and sat back in her chair.

"What happens tomorrow that didn't happen today or yesterday? What miracle will there be tomorrow? Will you stop the sun, or do you plan to do away with the Baron himself? Don't worry, no one listens around here, except perhaps you."

"I do not report everything you say. After tomorrow it won't matter; they won't be able to touch us."

"Did you come here to confide in me of your plan; am I to be trusted?"

"If you were not to be trusted, then . . ."

"Go on, tell me."

"Tomorrow I deliver a certain package to a certain man on a certain street corner. The man will give me the means of our escape to the Free Isles."

"What is in the package?"

"I risk the Burning House if I am captured with it; that is its value."

"You risk the Burning House? You must be infected or mad

or both." She laughed. "And you involve me in all this madness; you value my life as little as your own."

"You are not in jeopardy; you are not involved. I ask nothing from you; I offer you escape to the Free Isles if I succeed."

"The Free Isles," she said quietly, "Innisfree."

"The Free Isles," he said.

"Is there such a place?" she asked.

"Yes, there is. I know; we look for their agents daily. It is the sole threat to the Baron and we are enlisted to do naught but search out and kill members of their organization, the very same members who will ferry us away from this land of cancer and black rainbows."

"The Free Isles."

"The Free Isles. Just across St. George's Channel."

"Can it be so? Can I hope, dare I hope, Francis?"

"I can but try."

A red light began to pulse from the wall.

"I must go, my rest period is over."

"Yes, then . . . if I succeed, I will return here at noon tomorrow. Be ready to go, have everything you can carry prepared. Good-by."

"Godspeed. Wait . . . you didn't tell me what would be in the package."

"Our deliverance," he said. "Godspeed."

Q

Overhead the midnight gunship turned its rudder eastward and disappeared over the rim of the Fence. Its jet exhaust left silver chills in the night sky and reminded Francis of his destination, the quiet of his bunker. As an Agent he had been allotted a private bunker in the eastern quadrant far from the rim of the crater and the Regions of Quill. The clap of the iron gate brought him to his footsteps. Rearranging the limbs of the tree he activated the portal to his bunker. He skirted the anti-personnel monitor and switched on the No-Approach to his scanner. The recirculating device must have faltered from a power overload in the main Depot, for the room was hot and stale. He pressed the recycling switch and refilled the small bunker in a few moments.

He brought his coat out from the wall and reclined until he felt the hunger inside his stomach. Within the tin of synthesized meat he found a human hair. He almost laughed. He flopped down on his cot. Breeching the space in the wall, the panel showed an oncoming blip. One person on foot approached his perimeter and waited to be admitted. He called through the intercom. "Who is it?"

"Harlequain," came the rasping voice.

So it was that tubercular miscreant, Harlequain. He would have to let him in. After all he was a fellow Agent, and a refusal might arouse suspicion. He opened the Admit tube.

"My good man, Francis, may the leukemia never blight you."

"May you sire no three-armed dwarfs, Harlequain."

"How is your little friend?"

"My friend?"

"Rochalle of Distall's House."

"Do you know of her?"

"A little bird told me, Francis." The man's jowls flapped with laughter.

"A tacky job you did of that Greensby fellow," said Francis.

"Greensby? Greensby? I don't think I know the bloke."

"Here, I think this is yours." Francis handed him the strangling wire.

"Why, it does seem to have my initials on the handle. Can't afford to lose a good strangling wire every day. Where did you find it? Did I leave it here?" said Harlequain, egg crust on his eyelid.

"Found it in the Botanical Gardens, I did, in a stand of bamboo. Near Sussex Gardens," said Francis.

"Oh, I see." Harlequain coughed.

"Yes."

"Well, I won't tell Command about your little off-hour friend and you don't have to say anything about Greensby," Harlequain said, laughing.

"How much were you into him for? I'm curious," said Francis.

"More than money could help. You see, it had to do with his sister and the Burning House. . . ."

"You helped send her there, I suppose?"

"Well, after all, that is our business, to ferret out these spies from the Cannibal Islands. It was him or me; it just happened to be me this time. I followed him into the Gardens; what does it matter? You would have done him in anyway."

"True, however, I was ordered to question him first. The Superiors will be displeased. He had information concerning a quill plot."

"Don't worry, my compatriot," said Harlequain, rubbing his blunt fingers across his red-lipped mouth, "you're a top agent with many kills to your credit; they won't want to be too harsh with you. I even understand you're so much in favor with the Baron that you have access to the Archives. Is it true?"

"Perhaps," said Francis.

Harlequain pulled his chair up closer until Francis felt the impact of his horsefleshy face, bepocked and studded with the aftereffects of exposure to the Quill Region. Francis shuddered with the thought of that prohibited area; the Quill Region with its Burning House, the special project of the Baron where enemies too criminal for the favor of death were sent.

Harlequain broke into his thoughts. "Is it true what they say about the Weapon from the Spore?"

"The Weapon from the Spore?"

"Yes, yes, don't play games, Francis. The Weapon left by the vehicle from the Firmament after the Great War ended."

"Yes, it is there."

"Have you seen it? The weapon from the stars?"

"I have not seen it. To see it is to perish. I have seen its container. It is kept in the Archives' main vault."

Harlequain sat back. "You have seen it, then it does exist. I thought it was rumor started like the others to cower the people, but it does exist. And it can do all it is said it can do?"

"I have been told so by the Baron himself."

"You speak with the Baron . . . in conversation?" Harlequain said, wide-eyed.

"Yesterday I was made Advisor to the Baron on Affairs of Counter-Control."

Harlequain gasped. "You . . . ?"

"Yes, I."

"Earlier, I, I . . . didn't mean to try blackmail, sir, I only thought of . . ."

"No need, Harlequain, it is forgotten. Now will you leave me? I must gather my things together."

"You are leaving your bunker. It is such a nice location. You can see the crater lake from here and the lights along the Fence."

"Tomorrow I move to the Citadel; the Baron wants me close at hand."

"Oh, I see. May I be of any assistance?"

"No, thank you, I have a command patrol bringing a lorry over."

"Then, I take my leave, sir."

"Good-by, Harlequain."

Francis watched the blip fade from the screen and went about gathering his things, not for the trip to the Fortress but for a much longer voyage.

Q

Black snapping dragoons marched along the quayside, their prisoners prodded along with electrical pikes. They shuffled forward, heads covered with the customary black hood of those condemned to the Quill Regions. A red slash mark denoted the females, with two slash marks singling out the females with child. Their heads bent, they moved in a hunchbacked cadence that sent an icicle moth through Francis. The road was still pitted and cluttered with the debris of several wars; work gangs still toiled with their picks and shovels to clear it away. Most of them in their long gray robes were the chimeras indigenous to the Quill Region. Since most of the quill creatures had short life spans, new ones were constantly being trucked in from the detention camps. Completely denuded of hair, with transparent pale skin, and bright red under their nails and eyes, the things never failed to evoke a slithery feeling inside Francis. He maneuvered his motorbike through the line of marching prisoners and fired his pistol into the air to move a herd of quills who blocked his path. They slowly moved off to the shoulders of the road and resumed eating their rations. Their guard was being careless, thought Francis. The huge round eyes of the quill followed him; the high-pitched throb of their voices tore like little silver fishes at the chipped paint of his motorbike. All cleared away save one which sat on its haunches, crossing its forepaws across its chest. Francis fired another warning shot. The creature did not move.

Francis loaded a pain bullet into the cylinder and aimed at the fleshy portion of the underbelly of the quill. The bullet dug into the black fur and disappeared in front of its red tracer trail. The quill fell on its side, its limbs convulsing. It made sounds of pain as the bullet spun its way around before melting away harmlessly. Quills were protected by strict conservation laws and could not be indiscriminately killed, thus the issuance of the pain bullets. Some of its fellows dragged its moaning body off the road and Francis proceeded.

The early morning muted itself with a gag of tropospheric inversion; a mass of black smoke and ash hung over the city. Bright pelican lights were hung on the high-tension wires and gave off an amber diffuse glow, peppering the dismal sunlight. The air smelled like dirty oil to Francis. He replaced his breathing mask and goggles as he entered ground zero. Most of this section of the city still lay in gray puddles and would not be reclaimed for some time. A patrol gunship hovered over the sight of Parliament, machine-gunning a pack of wild sarks. Little puffs of smoke whipped up the dust along the rusting girders and blackened chips of concrete. Francis was at a safe distance and felt no qualms.

Blood-red distances and opal candlelights brought him to the crowning point of realization: the time of dagger-striking was at hand; the Weapon would be delivered whether his life was spent or not; he would meet death with a skeleton's grin. High toned and gleaming, the Citadel loomed at the top of the hill. Francis of North Dunnetowne presented his credentials, dismounted, and genuflected to the image of the Baron. A line of patrol craft lurked in the main courtyard being rearmed and refueled for another strafing run on the insurrectionist prisoners in Sussex Gardens.

Pembroke met him at the inner gate and clapped his hand around Francis' elbow, leading him deeper into the interior of the fortress. He had lost his own arm to the elbow to a quill when on a sterilizing mission to the nesting grounds of the creatures; he had been cornered and attacked. Now he wore the purple robe of Administrator and plotted statistical charts of the birth and death rates, production quotas, and so forth for the troops of laborers.

"Have you learned, Francis, the quill have joined the Insurrectionists?"

"The quill? Those cows and sheep? You must be sporting with me, Pembroke."

"I swear on the Rack. Intelligence has it that the quills have formed an alliance, arming themselves and attacking isolated outposts."

"But do they not have the mind of a squash; how is it that all this escaped us?"

"It is a mystery to me. No one imagined the quill could do else but eat, sleep, and reproduce. Well, use to reproduce; I took care of that problem."

"Is it all that serious?"

"More so, I'm afraid. There's a rumor that the Free Islanders are behind it all."

"And the Baron?"

"He wears his battle apparel today and carries a side arm wherever he goes."

"Do they fear for his life?"

"There is a plot afoot."

"Tell me more."

"No time, we meet with the Council; the Baron will address us."

Guards searched them as they entered the council rooms. Francis took his seat to the right of the Baron's throne and opened his brief case. The time lock functioned and the click of the rollers corresponded to the announced entrance of the Baron. Francis stood up with the rest of the council members and bowed.

The Baron wore the robes of combat, sparse and war trimmed. His imperial mask bore the tattooing of the sword and the shield in red and black. His side arm was his special two-handled model and hung heavily across his shoulders.

"Sit, gentlemen," he said. Much murmuring ensued until the Baron raised his armored gauntlet.

"Enough, you quail at the thought of battle. Your little voices scare the women and children, you comfort the enemy, and most importantly, you anger me. You see the empty regency seat; it was Compton of Norwich, the last of his line. Where is he now, you may ask? Where is Compton?" The Baron turned his head toward the captain of his guards. Francis viewed the half-breed with fear and suspicion. Some said that the Captain was half-quill, that his mother had been fathered by a quill bull. The Captain wore the mask of the Irretrievable, feathered in black and crimson. His words were rasping, his voice gnarled and slurred, and he smelled of death.

"The Burning House," he said.

Francis bore the news unperturbably. Compton had been his blood kin, yet he knew any sign of anger he might show would be his undoing. He felt the vulture eyes of the Captain burning through his mask into his own head.

"The Burning House," repeated the Baron. "Compton was found out. A conspirator and a traitor, he recanted his many crimes to me personally. They are too numerous to mention, but I may say you have that from reliable sources. He plotted the death of my cabinet members and tutored the Insurrectionists in their strategy of rebellion. And with Compton went his entire kith and kin to the Burning House. Women, children, maidservants, and manservants unto his sheep and cattle and quill. All."

All, thought Francis, stunned to the core of his being. Braybella and Curt, Sallon and Quasine. The twins, Sona and Praithe. Also the quill; how many had Compton kept, three hundred, four?

"Francis of North Dunnetowne," boomed out the voice of the Baron. "And you, kin of this man Compton, what have you to say?"

"I have no kin that is a traitor. I have nothing to say of this man. He is not."

"Well put, my wise advisor, well said. And for the rest of you? Any comment? Well and good. That is all I have to say, a small reminder to keep your heads up and warm blood in your veins. Go to your departments and see to it that nothing escapes your surveillance. I go to my men in the field. I take the battle to the enemy. You are dismissed."

The Baron exited the hall; no one stood until the Captain nodded the official dismissal. Francis felt his cold, reptilian eyes inspecting him as some piece of carrion, something about to die and soon edible.

Francis hurried to the Archives; perhaps in these first moments of relative confusion, he could accomplish his task, remove the Spore Weapon from its fetters and closet it away in the safety of his brief case. He made his way down the dimly lit cathedral halls to the inner sanctum of the Citadel, his heart pounding. He tried to think of Rochalle and the beauty of the Free Isles, but he could only feel the throbbing in his hand and the fear attendant to the Burning House. He felt wetness beneath his mask.

Suddenly Harlequain was at his side. He grabbed Francis at arm's length and spun him half around. "Beware," he whispered. "Much murder is imminent."

"What are you saying?"

Harlequain's eyes watered with near panic. "They are going to assassinate the Baron."

"They? Here? You must be mad."

"They are here on the grounds already. The Insurrectionists and quill. A suicide squad."

The sound of gunfire echoed through the corridors.

Harlequain squealed, "They're coming this way, run for your life."

Francis walked into the fusillade of bullets that turned his eyes back into his head. He felt himself drifting to the floor with Harlequain's faint screams sounding musical and quaint.

Q

Consciousness returned to Francis' shrunken brain valves with the absurd impression that milk was flowing out of his veins and staining the carpet of his father's house. But he had no father, no father's house, no father's carpet, but what was that if it were not milk? He wiped the warm wetness from his eyes and beheld the distorted water image of two luminous eyes, red-rimmed and staring into his face. It was a quill, and Francis instinctively reached for his side arm.

"Peace," said a voice. It was Pembroke's. With his good arm he helped Francis to his feet where he could see the staring eyes of the quill housed in the dead body propped up against the wall.

"The quill is dead, don't worry about it."

"And the others? What of the Baron?"

Pembroke laughed heartily and, almost whimsically, said, "The Baron lives. We killed all the intruders, but I'm afraid they took your friend Harlequain with them before they died."

"No prisoners?" Francis asked, rubbing his head.

"No. None would surrender. Be careful, a slight wound, but you know about infection, even the slightest wound could be fatal. But don't worry, we'll take you to the dispensary and I should think they will make you chipper again directly."

Francis knew that any hope of procuring the Spore Weapon would have to wait now. The sudden events had done away with all his plans for the moment. He would have to tell Rochalle.

Q

Bridling the current of his disquiet over the killings of his friends and enemies, Francis motored up from the coast road before the headlands at Bath. It was a quick journey and many a night's tryst had been spent there in the tenacious grip, the tight-breasted grip of Rochalle. Limpid pools of disused airfoils ransacked from the old airdrome crisscrossed the wide fields, where two or three trembling horses with yellowing teeth pulled at tufts of scrub. The rioters had run amuck that last June, when the soil turned to chalk. He drove an armored touring car with slits and alloyed turrets. Requisitions had issued him the vehicle from the main depot since he had top priority for cross-country travel. Moreover, the silo was located at Bath where Distall's House employed Rochalle. He made both business and pleasure a synonym and called the zigzagging road well even in the half-light of his black-out headlamps.

He swerved to avoid the lump in the road just as he rounded the curve on the outskirts of Bath. He thought it might have been a quill hit by a heavy van, but something made him stop anyway. He got out of his vehicle and approached the dark form in the center of the road, with his hand on his light machine pistol. The eye of the flashlight skittered over the gravel and asphalt to the spot where the form had lain. It was gone. Nor were there any blood tracings or the usual mucous marks of the quill. With no time to switch on his combat mask, he fired wildly when the cloth came over his head, blinding him and pinning his arms to his sides. Then he was clubbed into unconsciousness.

Q

He woke with his hand manacled before a large crackling fire. The night was moonless and pitch black; he could see people moving about at the fringes of the light. He smelled quill. The hair on the back of his neck hackled up. His head ached on either side and the pain his hand registered was excruciating.

Beats and twitters greeted his ears puffed from the pummeling; beats and twitters from a clutch of quill resting on their haunches facing the warm fire. They rocked back and forth on their huge heels and rubbed their forepaws in the warmth. He remembered Pembroke's knotted elbow stump and wondered at the size of their jaws. He became sickened with dread. Would they eat him alive or throw him into the fire for sport? From behind, someone lifted him under the armpits to a sitting position.

"Here, drink this, it will give you some strength. Go ahead, take it, man."

Francis squinted up against the bright glare of the fire into the face of a ruddy-faced man, yellow bearded and capped with a green and gold tartan.

"Bradley-Cooper, clan chief to this group of vagabonds and revolutionaries. And you are Sir Francis of North Dunnetowne, Advisor on Counter-Control. Here, let me undo your chains so we can shake hands."

Francis said nothing less he provoke some violent reaction from this madman; he knew little about these clan chieftains of the Quill Region. Obviously the man must be formidable since he had escaped the confines of the detention camp, much less traversed the terrain of the quill land.

"You look about you with much concern and disbelief; you see men and quill together. You doubt your senses."

"I am appalled. How can you bear to be near those reeking creatures?"

"Truly loathsome they may be until you make the pleasure of their company, but, after all, we do share a common ancestor."

"A biological verity, yet it makes them no less unappealing to me. Enough of this chitchat, Bradley-Cooper, am I to be held as ransom or merely offered up to your allies as a tasty morsel?"

"You haven't been kidnaped, and fear not about the alleged cannibalism of our friends, the quill. I am told by them that human flesh is most repugnant to them since most of it is tainted, contaminated, you know. Much like that wound on your hand."

"An old wound, not quite healed. It appeared in Nottingham last year."

"Never to heal, my friend. It is a symptom; you have the Scourge and I think you know it."

"Yes, I had wanted to go to Lourdes. . . ."

"Perhaps we have something here that may help. I'll ask the quill."

"The quill? What could those abominations possibly do or want to do for me?" Francis slumped back defeated and slightly annoyed at the same time.

The man gave out with a strange musical-like sound and soon a large quill was crouched before them, its huge eyes almost devouring Francis who flinched away.

Bradley-Cooper spoke amusedly, beginning with the same musical notes. "This is Lord Francis of North Dunnetowne. Now, Sir Francis, it would be difficult for me to translate the quill's appellation; it was that singsong sound I made at first. That's how they communicate. I'm learning a little of the vocabulary now; frightfully obtuse I am about it, though."

"Can it understand you and me?" Francis ventured to ask.

"It is a 'he' and he understands us implicitly and explicitly."

"You mean you can tell it to do things, carry supplies, perform amusing acts that we're all familiar with?"

"They are not beasts of burden, Sir Francis. They are quite intelligent, I dare say, superior to our own intellect; a forty per cent larger brain, more highly convoluted; three systems of communication including ultrahigh frequency. That lump on his snout is the center. It's very sensitive."

"They all have lumps on the snout; how do you discern the females from the males?"

"I do it by name, but for you it's just a matter of simple observation. The females of the species have slight swellings on their backs, somewhat like pods, and they don't have those short tusks the males do."

"I don't care to get close enough for the examination of their dental make-up."

"Actually, it's all irrelevant; they are bisexual and completely democratic with regard to themselves and their friends. With their enemies, it's quite another matter."

"I know, I've seen Pembroke's stump."

"Pembroke? I don't believe I know—"

"No matter. What *am* I here for then?"

"We would like to enlist your aid in the overthrow of the Baron and his tyranny. We want to restore the land as it was before the Devastation."

"As simple as that?"

"Quite."

"Do I have a choice in the matter?"

"Now, that's a bit sticky. Actually, you don't."

"Quite."

The man, Bradley-Cooper, sang out and the quill responded by settling itself heavily onto the ground facing Francis.

Bradley-Cooper spun off some musical sounds to the quill which seemed to ponder the words for a while before it jostled itself closer to Francis who held his breath from the stench. When the quill reached out two forepaws, Francis drew himself back against the tree behind him.

"Give him your injured hand," said Bradley-Cooper, much amused at Francis' dread. "It's perfectly safe. He wants to examine it and determine the extent of the putrefaction."

Francis hesitantly extended his own arm. He felt as if he had thrust his hand into a bowl of worms when the quill took it; he talked to take his mind off his revulsion. "I doubt if it, or he, can do any good at all for it; it's been some years in the making."

"Yes, I can see it certainly is no mere carbuncle," said the bearded man.

Francis screamed.

The quill had opened its huge wet jaws and thrust Francis' hand into the membranes of its mouth.

"Stop him," screamed Francis, in near panic and full disgust.

The quill extracted the now-wet, gummy hand from his mouth, looked at it sideways, and proceeded to drool an additional amount of its saliva onto the wound.

With a jerk Francis recovered his hand and held it by the wrist, too appalled to touch it.

"That's it," said Bradley-Cooper.

"What?" said Francis hoarsely.

"The cure; just as good as the one at Lourdes excepting you

don't have to fight all manner of monsters and bandits to get there."

"I see no transformation, only the same festering pit, but green now."

"Patience, it takes some time, this healing. Your mind must couch your body in a recuperative posture. Calm yourself. Now I'll leave you to your thoughts. He'll be your guard; trust you don't make any injudicious moves."

Left in the relative privacy of a half-ton quill, Francis found his situation ludicrous. Bumps of laughter began to peal from the back of his throat; he burst out laughing at the absurdity of his fettered fate. His explosion of merriment completely surprised the quill who fell backward in alarm before rolling his huge bulk upright. He regarded the man with curiosity, mused over the strange sound he had never heard before issuing from the man creature. He wanted to hear more of this strange man's music. The quill almost prodded Francis with a finger but restrained himself. When Francis broke out in peals of laughter again, the quill was ready and recorded every wave and crest of vibration for later examination and resynthesis.

Presently Francis lost interest in his laughter and grew quiet. Billows of smoke lip-curled up from the fire and fell among the feet of horses tethered to the command vehicle he had been driving. Cornstalks, dried and withered, were being bundled into the fire while a group of quill sat around the smoke. Francis was amazed; they were conjuring up images of animals and bizarre creatures out of the smoke. How they did this baffled Francis. They neither moved nor stirred from immobility yet very accurate renderings were produced in the swiftly escaping smoke.

"It boggles the imagination," said Bradley-Cooper as he approached Francis, communicating in that musical language to the quill that he was relieved of his guard duty. The quill lurched upward and ambled over to the group of his fellows where he sat down in the ring and promptly produced an exact replica of Francis in the broiling fumes over the fire.

"How do they do it?" asked Francis, as the quill's reproduction began shaking with laughter just as Francis had laughed moments earlier.

"Who knows? Perhaps the Royal Academy; I don't. I've seen them doing all manner of things which, very frankly, terrify me, but they are relatively meek creatures. Odd that we used to hunt them for floor furnishings and to light our lamps."

Out of the dark woods to the side of the encampment, an oscillating note wavered for a moment to be followed by a second, lower-pitched melody until both sounds merged into a consorted humming.

"And that?" asked Francis.

"Some quills mating, I imagine. Sounds like a pair this time."

"How do they manage with their great bulk?"

"I don't have the foggiest; never witnessed the act myself. They're very private about all that. Sometimes you can see their young protruding from their parent's stomach pouches; inhabit there for a year, I think. Quite cute little things, all bright orange hair and blue eyes when they're young."

"I thought all the quills had been sterilized under the Ecology Act."

"I thought the same, but somehow they worked around it. I've seen rolling herds of the little orange things scampering about the hills of the northern country, all bright-eyed and bushy-tailed. There, too, our army lies in the breech."

"Army? Have you massed forces?"

"On the sly we have, quite a few legions in all, some mechanized, but mostly weapons from before the Destruction: preserved cannon, a few meager missiles."

"Then it is true, the rumors rife of succor from the Free Isles. In the Citadel we were told that emissaries from Innisfree itself had approached the rebels with a covenant of alliance."

"I know little of such except certain munitions have been accepted by our leaders. As to a treaty, well, the quill probably know more about that than I. We are told no more than is absolutely necessary to forestall the power of the Baron's queries."

Francis watched mystified as the slouch angle of a quill's

sanguine tongue bored the base of the chestnut tree's uprooted trunk.

"What is it doing?"

"Milking the tree of its sap; a delicacy for them. They have a wide variety of consumables; eat almost anything. The quill that guarded you, for example; in appreciation for his having saved my scruffy life from a hazard patrol one night along the Fence perimeter, I gave him my gold medallion to wear. He looked at it and swallowed it right down, said his thank-you and sat down for the rest of the day digesting or contemplating it, whatever. They're very strange. Enough of the quill. Let us turn our attention to the question at hand, whether you lend us your seal or a nay; what's for?"

What was he to say to this dream of a nightmare decision? But what matter, the world might die at any minute and he would be just as lonely as scraps in a dog pile were to the kilns of the Burning House. He had learned never to take anyone into his confidence, thus the germination of his plot of escape for himself and Rochalle had been his doing alone. But that plan had proved untenable, for he needed the rebels as much as they needed him. He might just as well go corporate, he decided.

"My oath is given."

"That's it, man; so glad to have you with our little touring party. You can go now."

"Just go?"

"We'll contact you at the proper moment. Just go on about your business, kiss your sweet Nell for me. Ta."

Q

Francis felt quaggy; the only word he could think to describe the feeling of ooze at close proximity. He had the uncanny sensation, olfactory mostly, that a quill sat beside him as he hurried his plated vehicle toward the sulfurous lights announcing Bath.

Blithe and rugged, the sound alarm of his approach alerted the sentries who bustled about his vehicle; satisfied after their inspection, they waved him on with a warning to be vigilant for infiltrators and rogue quill that were bludgeoning outposts along the Outer Periphery. Francis drove the penchant for speed into the floor board where it bit the engine's crankshaft to revolutions beyond its capacity. With much smoke and clatter the vehicle stopped at the entrance of the gray, moated substation where Rochalle took her tenth days. He activated the alarm system on his command car and charged the detonators before entering the two-story mound of high-impact shielding. He descended two more stories under the coal-tar earth before he found the workroom where the technicians were attending Rochalle. She had her legs off and was directing the attention of the crew chief to an impacted electrode when Francis walked in unannounced.

"Francis, I asked you never to come here like this. It's poor manners confronting me like this. Is it so very urgent?"

"Have you forgotten so easily, the discussion of yestermorn?"

"But you specified the noon hour. It came and went without you, so I concluded there had been one of those unavoidable mishaps so common these days."

"I must talk with you alone; send the workers away."

"Prithee let me replace my legs. Do you like them? They're an old French motif."

"Very pleasing. I'll place myself in the anteroom."

"But a moment, Francis." She reached for her crimson hair on the stand next to the table as Francis ushered himself out to wait. She was not long in coming.

"Those legs were bothering me again; this was my only opportunity. You know how long it takes to get a good pair of legs; the backlog of orders at the Foundry . . ."

Francis' air of raw nerve endings wiped the frivolity away from her freshly implanted lips. "Whatever is the matter, Francis?"

"I have joined the rebels."

Rochalle looked quickly about. "No talk like that, Francis, or to be sure it's the Burning House for you."

"Verily, it is true. Just this eve I gave my pledge. I gave them my Blood Card before I left."

"You gave your Blood Card! They hold your life in their hands. How will you get your transfusions?"

"My cycle has just begun. I have a month before I will need a recycling. It was the test of my sincerity, the giving of the Card."

"I imagine you had little choice."

"Infinitesimal, yet I did it with some savor; the Baron is no great friend of mine. And, all in all, we may yet have our freedom."

"Freedom; who taught you that word? The rebels? The word forbidden by death for twenty centuries."

"It is not a profane word to my ears. Freedom means the Free Isles to me. No Burning House, no need to kill for a living, no crimes against the Baron or rules of Redeeming Social Values to tremble over in the morning. Perhaps my hand would heal there; the rebels said they may have a cure."

"No one heals any more, Francis. I learned that long ago, so I saved and hoarded and exchanged it all for this—this acrylic body. If I damage my hand, I order a new one. You fester."

"My body may be one large cancer, yet I still have that which you forfeited. I can die."

"Not here. It is forbidden. The Baron forbids it, the Law of Conservation."

"But in Innisfree—"

"You must get there first."

"I shall . . . and you with me, if you still care enough."

"You are with me, Francis. I made that choice, too, those years ago. Star-struck lovers we were, were we not?"

"We were."

"You are with me forever; your cytoplasm embedded here. We are part and parcel. And in your brain, too, a piece of me forever sown."

"I would retake those vows now."

"And I."

"Then let us make no flurry of words, halfhearted withdrawals from each other. If you have sworn your oath, mine is given, as well."

"As I had hoped, dearest Rochalle. We have but to wait for a message or courier from the partisans of the Quill Region."

"Is the time nigh for revolt; shall it come soon?"

"Anon, anon."

"Then let us waste no more of time, it hurries at my ribs. I feel a faint tide of sorrow rising in me, the future may hold its woe in withered arms before us and before I take it into my hands there are many caresses I would give to you, Francis of North Dunnetowne. Tomorrow I must resume my role as state harlot and the night is upon us greedily."

"My vehicle is at the ready, I shall take us to the nearest Conjoining Bunker at Trafalgar Square."

"I would take a few things with me."

As they left the dormant cone of the substation, the ashes of a thousand lives, dead a thousand years, settled around them.

"The weather is heavy tonight; the rain is bleak and coarse."

"It must be the winds; they blow from the American Sea."

"America, what was it like I wonder?"

As they lay enraptured with one another on the pallet in the select room Francis warranted as Advisor, Rochalle sighed and brushed her hair back.

"In but two years' time my role will be up, I can exchange this form for another more pleasing. Oh, how glad I will be to give back this crimson hair, these high hips, and this cough. They with their mad authenticity, their care for detail, their duty to the Past." She staggered a series of hacking coughs.

Behind the teeth of his worn mouth, Francis grinned and began to etch his words together. To the forefront they came since he could hold them no more from her.

"Rochalle. Tomorrow I take you to the Foundry, there to choose a new role, a new form for you, you need not wait two years."

"Can this be so? Please, not another disappointment."

"It is true; I have the power. In the morning you will rise and set and in the afternoon you shall rise once more."

"Let us sleep now, that the morning will come more rapidly. I bubble with excitement. Give me sleep, Francis."

"As you wish, Rochalle," he said, tenderly disconnecting her.

Q

Pembroke, with his stump swathed in the green and blue silk, his off-center eyes looking perennially askance, met them at the gateway to the Foundry with clearance tickets and fatherly charm.

"This is Rochalle, I take it?"

"Rochalle, this is Sir Pembroke, the gentleman who is making this all possible."

"I daresay, Francis; tut, tut, you'll embarrass me. Come hither, Rochalle, and make your choice. We have a new catalogue."

They entered the viewing room and seated themselves in the chairs while they were fitted with viewing modules.

"You'll note," said Pembroke with pride, "that we have added many new models to our collection since your last visit here. We've completely filled out our line of sixteenth- and seventeenth-century European styles and have even included notable vogues from twentieth-century Americana. There is a new Miss New York, a Miss Tokyo, and a Miss Moscow. Some of them are quite comely. Well, no more need to be said. We can begin."

As the devices were activated, a seemingly endless flow of subliminal images flashed through their minds as the scanners endeavored to exhibit all the Foundry had to offer. An hour had passed before all the roles had been viewed.

Pembroke rubbed his disjointed eye. "Quite an ordeal for the eyes. Well, my dear, have you found one to your liking?"

"I have," she said, looking toward Francis.

"Well, don't keep us up in the air, which one is it to be?"

"Set your viewers on hold. I've chosen catalogue number 20RW variant S."

"A fine year, a fine role. I remember it well; a favorite of that long-lost North American continent. We call her Miss MGM of 1970."

They all locked their viewers on the segment twentieth century until the digital dial stopped on the call letters.

"Yes, indeed," said Pembroke, "a bonny form it is indeed. One of our very favorites here. It's a designer's original, one of a kind and you have it. I am most enamored with it."

Rochalle smiled. "Do you like it, Francis?"

"I'm overwhelmed," he said.

"Yes, I think it will work well. The firm breasts, the small waist, the slim hips, the healthy lungs. We've caught the real flavor of those dear, dead days, two millennia ago."

"The hair is most pleasant, rather a blend of chestnut and flaxen," commented Pembroke. "A strikingly beautiful face, very uncommon mask, green-eyed."

"Most fetching," added Francis. "You chose most well, Rochalle."

"When can I have it, Sir Pembroke?"

"All in all, with the fittings and reorientation procedures, et al . . . if we start this afternoon, we can have you out and dancing in three days."

As Rochalle and Francis left the Foundry, she squeezed his hand tightly.

"Thank you, Francis. My cup runneth over."

"Rather bold you are, my dear, with your utterances."

"I felt it appropriate. Something I remembered from my previous role at the nunnery—for the historical plays, you remember."

"I labored under the misconception that previous roles were completely removed from your consciousness upon refillment."

"Generally so, but I've always had a faculty for retaining at least some memories even after recycling."

Outside, she stopped on the steps. "I must go now. Sir Pembroke waits for me."

"In three days I will return for you," said Francis sadly.

"Yes, here, take my ticket stub, you may not recognize me." She smiled.

"Hardly, I could recognize you in any guise."

"Come, child," said Pembroke, "we must be on time. The Foundry waits for no man."

"Until later." They touched fingertips.

"Good-by, Francis."

"Thank you, Sir Pembroke."

"It is nothing, nothing, Sir Francis."

Francis watched the two figures disappear beyond the obsidian doors.

Q

A melancholy, wheatless wind swept shudders through his frame as he entered the Quill Region on his return from Bath and his chambers in the Citadel. With his running lights he could still make out the jagged rim of the great crater to the south and the sterile waters it contained. A patrol gunship sank down like a spider from the mold-hued clouds, scanned his vehicle, and hid itself back into the vapors again. The dilapidated hovels housing the quill stretched in their unvarying architecture into the distance; long, corrugated sheds, policed by heavy gun crews and squads of brindled, razor-toothed sarks, culled from the great offshore trenches. The only natural predator of the quill, their kennels were always close to any quill compound, the din of their shrieking howls cutting the flaccid air to ribbons, their coils and fangs hanging from their fur-streaked bodies which scuttled about crablike, always in clusters of five or six, kept in rein by their handlers. Any quill outside his shed after the imposition of curfew was left to the sarks. Often the bones of a quill, usually the huge femurs, were brought back by the sarks and left on the doorsteps of their handler's billet.

Francis passed, unimpeded, through the center of the complex. As he came upon the enclosure for the political prisoners, his skin began to crawl. Rising up into the mercuric sky vapors, the dun-colored smokestack blinked with red warning lights. Around it, the sheds that fed the smokestack huddled as for warmth, for the great chimney was always warm. Beneath it, in the lower phlegmatic bowels of the earth, beneath the greasy top soil, dwelt the Burning House. Francis hurried to his room and showered for a long time.

Political dogma was like so many whiffle balls, Francis thought, as he stood in the gallery waiting for his audience with the Baron. Dry ice ran through his hands, his fingernails fogged with many fears. Had he been discovered? Clamshells clamped their brilliantine arms around his eye nerves and dragged his hopes for freedom down into the abysmal depths of the deep black carpet on which he sat. He came up for air only with the thought of Rochalle in his mind.

He gave courtesy to the Baron and the Captain and breathed more easily. The conversation turned to local amenities such as weather, state of health, and gaming luck. The Baron wore an informal mask of green and cobalt blue, while the Captain wore a muted gray affair with opaque eye shields. Some said that the Captain had no face, that it had been lost in combat when he was a fusilier, or that the Captain's hybrid nature had produced a face too horrible to behold. Francis relaxed when the Baron offered a glass of rare pre-spore brandy. He sat behind the huge desk hewn from a solid block of petrified wood, with a bank of communicators at his elbow. The Captain sat to the left in a straight-back hanging chair which swiveled disconcertingly. Francis felt his eyes, though concealed by the opaque eye pieces, slowly rotating with the retrograde motion of the chair. An infernal itch prickled under his mask, onto his scalp, and crept into his nose and throat like some invisible odor. Breastbones and feather-tastings stole their way into the conversation that Francis only half-heard. He was still stunned by the cordiality of the proceedings; the Baron and his archexecutioner sipping old brandy with him as if nothing were out of the ordinary.

"Extraordinary," said the Baron.

"What . . . ?" fumbled Francis.

"Extraordinary, I said, the news we have from the Free Isles surveillance."

"You must mean the rumors concerning direct aid to the rebels."

"No, Sir Francis, I refer to the reportings that the Free Isles are sinking into the sea. History repeats itself."

"What?"

"Comical, is it not? Our enemies merely sinking into the ocean like paper boats drowning in the Wednesday wash. Some geological abnormality, volcanoes erupting beneath the sea, earth's crust shifting. It appears only Innisfree still peeks above the surf; all the other isles have settled some fathoms down. Only Innisfree. Sad, I'm genuinely moved to some emotion, I believe. Quixotic, paradoxical, amusing sensation to say the least. I may have to visit the Burning House, lay a wreath or dedicate some of the condemned to the memory of the Free Isles. What do you think of that, Captain?"

"Very good, sir; perhaps a quill or two."

"Perhaps. They make good kindling."

Francis' hopes became a slag heap dripping into the bottoms of his boots. The Free Isles gone by a freak of nature. A dwarf of nature, a mutant of nature. Now everything was the same. That common denominator, the great cosmic joke, had shattered everything into mad laughter.

"The prophets had warned of it, if I remember correctly. We'll have to set some of them free; they may be of some service after all."

"Sire," said the Captain, "I took the liberty of having the last prophet sent along with the other curios to the Spore Federation as gifts."

"Alas and alack, I'm sure they've dissected him by now."

"Sire, not to interrupt, but have I been called for some particular reason?" asked the dismayed Francis.

"Are you anxious to leave our company so soon, my Sir Francis?"

"My consort is to be reissued her new role today and I must meet her at the Foundry at noon."

"Oh, then you must be anxious to see her new form. Pembroke tells me it is most attractive. I shan't keep you too long. The Captain tells me you've returned your strangling wire and dagger. Is this true?"

"In my new capacity as Advisor, I thought I would have little use for such items."

"But, my dear Advisor, the killing must go on. True, you will not be called upon to dispose of lesser obstacles as in the past, however, we do have a list of rather imposing individuals, some advanced in the hierarchy, whose conduct leads us to believe them not wholly sincere. A number of provincial commandants, a few members of the security establishment, even a council member or two. These are special cases deserving and requiring unusual tact and aplomb. We can't have just any agent handling these ticklish affairs. We need a man of your integrity and experience."

"Is there any case you have in mind at the moment, sire?"

"Yes, the Commandant of the Burning House is a point in fact."

Francis felt his lower intestine jerk.

"We have it from reliable sources that this rather foolish man has been allowing prisoners to escape. One of his lieutenants made the initial accusation, a good lad, from a fine lineage. You'll meet him at the camp. He is our liaison man now in lieu of an agent. On such short notice though, we feel that action should be taken immediately in light of the special problem . . . requiring a final and prompt solution. So, there it is, I leave the disposition of the case in your hands. Here is your strangling wire, your dagger. Use them in good health. May the pox never scar you."

"May your children be blessed with fertility," Francis answered automatically. "Excuse me, sire. . . ."

"No need to apologize, the thought was well meant."

The Captain came down from his perch and made an unswerving line to the heavy chest in the center of the room. "The Spore Device, now, sire?"

"Yes, Captain, carry it here. Sir Francis, another moment of your time. Here before you rests the Spore Device; I take you into our confidence. Perhaps you heard us mention the Spore Confederation. Another ship is approaching our planet; it appears some Eonic cycle has been set into motion again. We've sent offerings and felicitations. I believe that the potency of this particular device in our possession has in some way weakened and must be replaced, thus the return of the Spore Vessel. Is that the consensus of opinion, Captain?"

"Yes. It appears to be a two-thousand-year cycle."

"So, there you have it; momentarily we expect our visitors. With all this turmoil about the land, it hardly makes for a proper reception. So I have implemented plans to secure the equilibrium of the country as speedily as possible. You have been assigned your portion, as have all of us. I'm sure you realize the importance of maintaining the enormous advantage we have with the Spore Device in our keeping. There are many who might very much relish that power. Moreover, I still do not entirely discount the Free Isles. With Innisfree still intact, our enemies there will do all within their power to accommodate themselves to the Spore Device with all manner of guile and subterfuge. So, for now, Sir Francis, do take care of the blight in our sight and remove the blemish from our land, the Commandant."

"When is this to be done?"

"Immediately," rasped the Captain.

"And my consort?"

"She will be brought to your chambers."

Q

Francis left the Citadel, a life-size puppet with his thoughts disembodied by a hundred miles. To kill the Commandant of the Burning House, who was guilty—guilty?—of releasing prisoners, would be interpreted as a signal of his defection from the rebel cause, and they had his Blood Card. On the other hand, if he did not perform the task just ordered, the Baron would have him sent to the Burning House. And what of Rochalle? The House of Reconciliation for her. He would have to do it and explain it later. Besides, the Commandant might be working without the collaboration or knowledge of the rebels and so would not be missed.

Why was he doing any of these loathsome deeds? he asked

himself. What reward could he expect? The Free Isles were soon to be no more or so the Baron attested and the Baron had no reason to lie. Innisfree tottered on the brink of volcanic extinction; its pinnacle of frozen lava easily snapped twiglike by the convulsive heavings of the ocean floor. All for chance, all for the "great maybe," he thought. Hope wreaked its slavering jaws on the mock holiday of Francis' dry riverbed, settling the dust of utter despair so that he could trod on the gulch-hewn path to the carrot of pleasure held out by the rabbit skeleton of death's accomplice, grinning life. He steered past the broken rib cages of ancient buildings, over the five-mile mount of earth, the mass grave of half a million people who lay in shards and pieces in the burial crater. The metal Obelisk bore the now worn and illegible names, buried in common, centuries before—the graveyard at Piccadilly Circus.

The unclaimed areas near the protection of the Fence bounding the Quill Region were riddled with gaping holes. Some of the craters had become filled with ozone and water, others had been used for burials, some more recently had been domed over and hermetically sealed. These were the new government developments, part of the prosperity program initiated by the Baron. Trees and shrubs were being carted down from the unaffected regions of the north and planted; trainloads of grains and flower seeds were being distributed and sown over the scarred tissue of the land. But the sunlight could not penetrate the thick envelope of ash and debris that still filled the upper atmosphere. Dispersal machines were being set up at key installations in an attempt to clear the air, but these seemed to be more rumor than fact. The gray city fled before him as he approached the site of the Burning House. He entered the camp and was met at the headquarters building by the young Lieutenant the Baron had mentioned.

"A pleasure to meet you, Sir Francis."

"The pleasure is mine; the Baron speaks favorably of you."

"He is too kind. I merely performed my duty when the scandalous affair came to my attention," he said humbly, yet sparks danced in his cold blue eyes beyond the military mask.

"And the Commandant?"

"I fear he knows. He is in his quarters now. Perhaps we should apprehend him before he makes his escape."

"Where would he go?"

"Perhaps the Free Isles? Others have gone before him."

"Yes, Lieutenant, perhaps the Free Isles. Where are his quarters?"

"This way."

For the first time since he had entered the compound, Francis let his senses function. The clouds over the camp bore the imprint of countless agonies, and actually seemed to moan and heave in a futile attempt to free themselves from the grip of the Burning House's barbed tower. The windows of the prisoners' shed were like vacant eyes, the smudged white walls had the sickly sheen of starving flesh. The very ground itself quivered. And a hundred feet beneath, the Burning House churned out its product.

"This is his door. Shall I knock?"

"I think not, Lieutenant."

Francis kicked open the door, with weapon drawn and death projectiles armed.

The Commandant, tall and gaunt, stood up from his desk, facing them. Francis stepped through the doorway, the young Lieutenant at his side.

In some other voice, the words, "This doesn't make any sense," jumped into the brain of Francis just as the huge shadow swept across the Lieutenant. Francis fired instinctively; the quill fell dead with the Lieutenant's arm still in its jaws. With his free hand the officer blew his call whistle just as the Commandant made his dash through the door. Sarks, alerted by the call of the whistle, intercepted the Commandant in the center of the campgrounds. Before their terrified handlers could call them off, the Commandant littered the field and blew away in the hot sticky wind.

Q

"Well done, Sir Francis. It could be called an unfortunate accident," said the Baron. "Just to add credence we shall have the sark handlers executed. Too bad about the Lieutenant. How does he fare?"

"Well," said Francis, "I think he was most grateful when he learned you had given special permission for him to relinquish his body for an Automatic. Pembroke tells me the Foundry is making up an exact copy of the Lieutenant's body. He is well pleased."

"Good. I think a citation is in order for him also, let the people know of one of their heroes. I'll have my media secretary manage that. Well, I think that's enough. Go now, Sir Francis, go to your chambers, some lithesome wench awaits you with baited breath."

"Thank you, sire."

Q

Francis left the chamber, quickly, still with that disturbing feeling that some evil spirit attended his every move. Breathless with a creeping anger, Pembroke met him in the corridor.

"I must talk to you, Sir Francis. It's very urgent."

"Not now, it must wait." With that Francis hurried away to his chambers without looking back into the distraught face of Pembroke.

Q

"Rochalle," he whispered dumbstruck. He could not move, paralyzed with the vibrations of her new body. "Is it really you I see before me?"

"It is I." She smiled. Her skin was tanned appropriately to match the gloss of the svelte suede smoothness of her long, slim legs and green inlaid eyes. The timbre of her body set his senses burning; the call of her wide-lipped mouth tore him asunder and he rushed into her embrace.

Some time passed before he could form his words. A fine

threaded canopy of peace covered his thoughts from the wire brush of fear and hope that scraped at his consciousness. He was overwhelmed by the beauty of her body, inundated past all logic, all reasoning, all thought. Gone were the bruises and scars, the chancres and discolorations of the previous Rochalle. In its abused and misused place a perfect form lay in grace.

"Francis," she said, "I have something to tell you. We do not have the three days of rest and readjustment as usual—"

"But, it is always so, they have no right—"

"Calm yourself; the Baron has told me that although I am of the female category, I am freed from my lease. I do not have to return to the Distall House or any house nor must I serve any function than that of serving you, of being your companion unhindered by any other obligation."

"The Baron said this?"

"He told me to give you the news at a proper moment."

"It is all too incredible. Why does he do this?"

"It is my thinking that he has you singled out for a Regency post."

"It is some quirk of fate; I who plan his—" Something made him hold back his words, perhaps the thought of a hidden microphone. His new surroundings were more lavish than his private bunker but certainly less private and more easily monitored.

"What?"

"Nothing that merits repetition." His mouth felt stale and some pain in his hand struck him a chill draft; he felt off center, in some uncomfortable imbalance.

"Rest," she said. "Rest, Francis."

He fell into a troubled sleep where laborers were erecting a great stone sarcophagus on which eagles with bloody beaks turned their backs to a cold and wintry squall moving across the Channel. He heard bagpipes in some far distant room, some reclamation center loudspeaker called out names and numbers. A gallery of faces passed before him; places, cities, all in a flood of unintelligible words and languages. He smelled the sluglike odor of the quill, felt cold iron around his neck, and wrestled with the ghosts of Harlequain, the Commandant, and oddly enough, the old Rochalle with her high hips and coughing in his face.

Q

Weeks passed.

Hungry brain bags from the far swamps, luminous jelly and batlike, floated through the city as the heated streets gave off their names in random fashion. Francis knew the narrow road-ways like the veins on the back of his hand. He had hoped to reach the terminal before the weekly train set off for Clacton-by-the-Sea. Porters were carrying the bags to the platform as he arrived. A quill, bent and grayed, swept the pathways clear of the ash that fell heavily. Although its tusks and glands had been removed by law, Francis made a wide circle around the lumbering behemoth.

Steam poured from the wheels of the stale-colored locomotive, blistering the paint on the concrete abutments and walls covered with myriads of names and dates, epitaphs, greetings, and curses scribbled on the walls centuries before when the already aged subway system had served as emergency bunkers. It had been left as a reminder.

Francis knew that if the Clacton train had not disembarked, then Rochalle's express had not entered the hangar. People around him stared; he felt self-conscious and held the bouquet behind his back. The people stared at the flowers; some children ran up and touched the petals, darting away with giggles. Francis blew the flakes of ash from the red and green blossoms, adjusted more protectively the film of tissue paper about the precious bouquet. He looked warily about; the ravenous brain bags were hanging overhead in the shadows.

A class of Series II school children visiting the subway made guesses as to the names of the flowers. "Plastic," adjudged their teacher-guard. She bore the purple blotches on her throat and face; Francis could feel her disease. The troop of school children, harnessed into two parallel lines, moved off down the tunnel with a tug of their restraining straps. One of the children in the rear had dropped in his traces and was simply dragged along with the hundred others. He would be cut loose and separated when a restroom was reached. Perhaps, thought Francis, the child had been careless and an errant brain bag had settled over its head. They roosted in the Citadel battlements and were the devil to dislodge. One just learned to live with the brain bags, being careful when one walked, eyes wary of the sky overhead.

Just then the children in the lead let out with horrendous screams. The livid-faced teacher dashed back past Francis calling out the warning, "Brain Bags!" Joining the hue and cry, as any citizen would, Francis followed her back to the place she directed. It appeared that a lone brain bag had squeezed through the ventilator shaft, from which it flung itself on the head of one of the youngsters, a girl of seven or eight operations. Crumpled like a marionette, stringless and limp, the child's body was encircled by her curious classmates who pointed and conjectured while the brain bag, bloated after its meal and satisfied for the moment, not immediately dangerous, bobbed to the ceiling.

Suddenly a second chorus of children's screams echoed through the shaft; the maintenance quill had somehow broken its tether and stood beneath the hovering brain bag. Bedraggled of fur and shaking with age, the quill raised its forepaw to the brain bag and brought it down from the ceiling. Everyone present gasped when the quill opened its huge jaws; Francis saw the toothless cavern. All witnessed as the quill popped the brain bag whole into its mouth and swallowed.

"At least they're good for one thing, those disgusting quill," said the teacher. Her shrill voice broke the silence, onlookers and children alike dispersed. Francis waited to see what the security guard would do to the quill. When the guard did approach the quill, who did not protest, he merely took up the tether chain and led the creature back to its post at the rear of the platform.

Francis followed the guard, relieved that no harm had been meted out to the quill. "It was kind of you not to punish the quill. He performed a service by removing the brain bag; the children were endangered," Francis said to the rumpled uniform of the guard, who leaned against the sign reading Charing Cross Station.

"Why punish it? It can hardly hold up a vacuum. In two days' time the wagon from Economics will come around for him. You know the Baron's new beautification program? All the new shrubbery and flowers being planted?"

"I've heard."

"Well, old disposable quill are at a premium, going for ten quid a pound in the black market."

"Why so?"

"Fertilizer. They make cracking good mulch, they say."

Francis looked in the direction of the quill who turned its head as if it had been listening; it resumed sweeping the ground with the vacuuming machine. The wind of the train from Dover blew a swirl of ashes obliterating the form of the quill. From the ashen mirage of the old quill, Francis' attention focused on the passengers stepping down from the third car. He closed his eyes and concentrated on the section of Rochalle's tissue implanted in his hypothalamus, deciding to let it function as a directional device to indicate when Rochalle was near. He waited for a response.

When nothing happened, and the fading sound of footsteps informed him that all the passengers had left the train, he opened his eyes with worry.

"What were you doing, Francis?" said Rochalle who stood in front of him.

"Oh"—he laughed—"were you standing there the entire time?"

"I was." She saw the bouquet. "Flowers," she said. "How beautiful. How strange. They must have cost much; they're very rare."

"Just a silly thought I had; it's not important. How was your holiday?"

"Wonderful. The ocean was like spun glass; no, no, more like liquid jade. Oh, I don't know, it was beautiful except you weren't there with me to enjoy it."

"The Citadel keeps me well busy. A holiday . . . well, I may never have another with all this responsibility. I never wanted it."

"All great men have felt the same."

"Great men? I—" with sudden darkening, Francis clipped out, "I, a minor assassin with a persistent rot? I, a great man? Your words bring home to me the truth of it all. These last few weeks have been so calm and uneventful, I've lulled myself into a complacency. I've grown fat on the blood and pain of greater men than I ever could be."

"I call it honor, pride."

"I call it filth, wretchedness."

"Now, now, Francis, it's good that I returned early. I see you need care and comfort."

"Yes," said Francis, rubbing his temples, "yes."

"Take me home and let me ease your disquiet. Take my hand. Is that not better?"

"Yes . . . better. I'll call for the vehicle."

Q

Months passed.

Months that passed in the arms of the new Rochalle caused Francis to develop a paunch, but the festering hole in his hand closed and a healthy scab had begun to grow. He had killed no one in some time, had mostly attended the various park dedications and horticultural exhibitions as the representative of the Baron. For some reason the reptilian nausea of the Captain was absent from the Baron's side where Francis now found himself. The Captain had disappeared from sight around the time of the spring equinox. New things were coming into bloom, things sprouted, birds were reported seen in Leicester, but it was not confirmed elsewhere; even the dangerous but colorful brain bags were mating high in the cubby-hole rafters of the Citadel. New proclamations had eased many of the restrictions imposed during the war alert, people were appearing in the streets, the ash level had fallen sharply. All in all, breathing lightly of the new intoxicating breeze, Francis' malaise had long since lifted, his spirits buoyant.

"There is a possibility that I may be granted a travel visa." Francis smiled over breakfast of crumpets and whey.

"Truly?" said Rochalle, pouring the tea into the porcelain cups. "To where, may I ask . . . if it is not a state secret?"

Francis paused before he answered, still mesmerized after all these months by Rochalle's beauty. He could feel his eyes cloud over with every glance he took of her, from every lutelike word she uttered.

"Then it is a state secret?" she asked.

"No, no, dear. I was just enraptured—"

"Please, Francis, you'll make me color."

"State secret, but of course not. Innisfree."

"Innisfree?" The excitement shone in her richly appointed eyes.

"Relations have so mellowed since the disastrous destruction of most of the island chain, that virtual peace has been brought about. We even have plans to send medical supplies, food, technical assistance to the people of Innisfree. In fact, our cricket squad has been invited over to take part in the championship games held in Innisfree."

"It is a good omen, is it not?" she asked.

"Most assuredly. And I am to go with them, rather, we are to accompany them."

"We?"

"Yes." He smiled.

"Can I believe what I hear? Our first holiday together. It will be marvelous."

"Accommodations have been made, all is in readiness. We train to Dover, then the hydrofoil to Innisfree."

"I take it we leave soon."

"Monday, a week."

"Oh, Francis, you tell me so belatedly; I shall never have time to prepare myself, the packing alone—"

"No need to transport our entire estate, we only stay a week."

"A week?" She gasped. "A week is two thousand years. What am I to do?"

"I feel confident that you will manage it quite well. Especially with the new tri-wheeler I have waiting for you outside."

"What? My own tri-wheeler? Outside? Oh, this is all too much for me. I was never designed for this much excitement."

"You'll fare well. But I must go now; the Baron has called for me. Most likely a new persimmon plantation to bless."

"Good-by, darling." She flung her arms around him.

"Oh, hmm, well, yes, I must be off."

"A kiss."

"A what?"

"A kiss. Here."

"Where did you learn that?"

"I've been spending much time in the Archives, going back into the data files on the era of my body. Some very pleasant trivia I've learned. I've viewed all the histories that survived the Punishment."

"Well, the results of your scholarship are most pleasant. We'll have more later."

"At your convenience, m'lord." She curtsied.

Q

What of Bradley-Cooper? What of the Quill Insurrectionists? The distant memories appeared in the windshield of the command car Francis maneuvered around the Grotto; the wipers blurred them away in the melted rain, viscous with ash and glowing pollen. It was the noctiluscent variety, wafted in from the gardens of Innisfree, glowing violet and vermilion. It took a chance stream of upper-sphere wind to carry it the distance. It happened infrequently; this the second in Francis' recollection since the rumors of the Spore's second coming. Legend and deviant said that the appearance of the luminescent grains meant a bountiful year or heralded the birth of a great leader. The brain bags had gone berserk as did happen with the influx of the tasty pollen and could be seen zipping about through the diaphanous clouds of glowing purples and reds filling themselves to the bursting point with the delicacy. Because of their transparent skin, the brain bags became colored lanterns filling the night with globes of glowing color. Appeased by their swollen bodies, the brain bags were not likely to seize anyone's head, so crowds of people emerged from their dwellings to view the spectacle. The wind seemed to change directions; the mass of flying-fire brain bags were carried over the Quill Region where they remained hanging and soaring for the remainder of the night like beacons.

Francis found his mind working in diagrams and charts: the brain bags scoop up the pollen; the quill eat the brain bags; the poorer peasants roast the tasty quill; the Baron taxes and tortures the peasants; the Spore threat intimidates the Baron; Time and Space must control the Spore, for they can come in their space craft but once every two millennia. His mind telescoped back to his own meager being, now so small after the geometric progression it had just exercised. But, in himself, Francis felt heartier, more secure, philosophic. His lot had improved considerably, obviously, he told himself. See, you even have leisure for delving into philosophy, mental gymnastics, and studied reflection. A promotion seemed forthcoming. Perhaps a Regency post.

But, what had happened to Bradley-Cooper and the army he had waiting in the wild mountains? Perhaps they had all been ferreted out and dealt with. Perhaps, yes, perhaps that would explain the long absence of the Captain. He would be in command of any operation in the rugged region bordering the Quill Region for he knew the terrain well, had been born there, bred by the woman and the he-quill.

Driving through the impoverished countryside, Francis saw the signs of progress being made under the Baron's program. Farmers were harvesting their crops, planted the previous spring with the aid of the tractors and reapers still shiny from the Foundry, which had been retooled for the production of farm and industrial equipment, no longer producing the Automatics except on a limited scale. It was fortunate that Rochalle received the new body before the cutback had been effected.

What had brought about the softening of the repressive measures and the burgeoning concern for the average person, Francis did not know nor could he guess what forces had influenced the Baron to act so favorably. He brought his vehicle into his parking rectangle and let himself into the foyer of his chambers. He had the better part of an hour before his appointment with the Baron, appointments becoming more and more common the last few weeks. The Baron had been asking him all manner of questions concerning the thoughts of the people, the trends he perceived, and the most efficient ways of meeting the problems of the land. Quite early in the discussions, Francis had been so bold as to recommend a cessation of the monthly reprisals against the quill population for the abortive uprising the year previous. When the Baron declared general amnesty to all concerned, Francis was emboldened to make more daring and far-reaching suggestions, and the Baron had listened and often enacted them. Mating among the quill was no longer a capital crime. Cuts in the military budget were transferred toward research and development in the fields of medicine, agriculture, and consumer goods. Children were not weaned from the Formulation Plants quite so early as before, and when the charts on crime and psychological abnormalities declined, the period was even further extended. Francis found himself more than ever involved with the populace and their problems, spending more and more time in the Archives and on the road conducting his own investigations. Completely unannounced, he visited the leukemia colonies where he uncovered and eliminated much graft and corruption which resulted in improved conditions for the thousands of sufferers who were still, unfortunately, required to remain in the isolated regions. The deformed were no longer treated as outcasts and plague carriers. Widespread reforms raised them from subquill status to that of citizens having the protection and aid of the Baron himself. A new treaty with Innisfree was about to be signed, with Francis attending; no new outbreaks of violence had been reported for months; and, most dramatic of all, the closing down of the Burning House. True, the young Lieutenant was kept there to oversee the vast camp, but its chimney stack no longer befouled the air and the soul with its grisly pollution. Perhaps it was truly the Dawn of the New Age.

Francis had everything packed and delivered to the Port, yet a thousand items flashed through his mind. What had he forgotten and left behind, had he remembered all the details prerequisite for their departure for Innisfree? He opened the door for Rochalle who had been waiting on the main steps of the Citadel for him to arrive. She got in, breathless with excitement.

"Are we really going, Francis?"

"I would wager ten to one that we are."

"Do you have everything? All the papers; a good supply of blood for yourself? You were lucky to get a duplicate Blood Card. And your good mask, did you bring your formal mask?"

"Yes, yes, yes. Pray you end this interrogation or I'll set you off on a barnacle by yourself, and you can question the waves to your heart's content."

"I am sorry, Francis, but I'm so elated over this fabulous adventure."

"You must learn to conduct yourself with a deportment befitting an ambassador's wife. Calm yourself."

Rochalle said nothing, but he could feel his words making their way home.

She cried out loudly, flung out her arms so wildly that he feared they would wrench themselves loose from her body. "Ambassador!?"

"Ambassador to the Free Isles, to the court of Innisfree. The Baron pinned the red sash on me this afternoon."

"How wonderful for you, Francis."

How ironic, he thought, that, after all, he had managed his way to the Free Isles in a manner he had never dreamed. From plotting the murder of the Baron to occupying the seat of honor on his right side; the thought came as a swooping brain bag splattered against the vehicle's protective windshield. He turned on the heavy-duty wipers and sprayed the remains away.

"No brain bags to plague us in Innisfree," he said.

"No Baron, either."

"How can you disparage our benefactor?"

"Easily. The irony of this whole turnabout does not escape me, Francis. Has there not been any word from the partisans? Do they still not muster their forces?"

"I know nothing of their plans, their whereabouts, or their forces. In fact, I doubt seriously if they still exist at all, rather much more likely sank into oblivion under the sea of broken cities."

"Like the Free Isles?"

"Somewhat."

"I met a prophet in the streets outside Bath when I went to market yesterday," she said, her words slow and thoughtful.

"Yes, you met a prophet . . . ?"

"And this very old and sage gentleman spoke to me a parable. He said, 'When there is not a whole man on the throne, the Free Isles will rise from the sea as great fires descend from the heavens. A son born under the signs of air and fire will unseat his own father for a greater glory.' And he also said, in passing, 'The Baron will die, long live the Baron.'"

"Did you pay him for his hoary words, told a thousand times before by lesser prophets?"

"A gold sovereign."

"I fear, my dear Rochalle, your prophet was but a clever fellow, for it is known to me that the last prophet was sent as a gift to the Spore Federation."

"But he said he came from the Quill Region where prophets were still venerated and protected."

"Very unlikely, but perhaps . . . there are many strangenesses about the quill we are just beginning to uncover."

"You spoke of the Spore. Will they arrive soon? I would like to meet one."

"They've come and gone."

"What? No mention was ever made."

"True. Only this afternoon did I myself learn of all that had transpired. They came to the Citadel without use of any vehicle. They entered the Fortress unannounced and unseen, made their way in the Archives, and removed the Device, replacing it with another. It appears they had some words with the Baron, although who 'they' are, what 'they' present to the eye, I do not know. Whatever, they seem to be the direct cause of all the new legislature."

"What did they say?"

"I don't know. The words must have been powerful, for they humbled the Baron."

"Will they return again?"

"In some way I do not think they will ever leave."

"Things are happening so rapidly, Francis. Stop the spinning earth, hold it steady for me, I grow fearful."

"There is no time to be fearful, we draw nigh unto the Port." The escort vehicles peeled away as Francis' driver made directly for the loading ramp.

Arm in arm, Francis and Rochalle walked up the gangplank while quill porters carried up their trunks.

"See there, quills working for wages, being paid for their labor; no longer slaves," said Francis proudly.

The stateroom was decorated by the Baron's designer and gave excellent views of the sea and surrounding docks. On the entrance table a bottle of iced champagne crackled.

"The note reads: 'Best wishes from the Baron.' A bottle of champagne?" said Francis quietly, shaking his head. "Flowers, champagne, a trip to Innisfree, all the dreams never answered of millions of people and they shower upon us."

"You have done much; you deserve these tributes."

"I am a pinpoint in the world of blackened ash, nothing more. These trophies are of someone else's life, I know him not. Shall I seek him out and return all this bounty? Surely there has been some great comic error, some mistaken address, a faulty bead on Fate's abacus. The numbers are upon me, I take them in threes and sevens." Francis stopped speaking. Behind him something breathed great volumes and exuded those odors he knew too well. He spun around. There, standing in the door with a trunk case, stood the old quill Francis had encountered in the train terminal months earlier. When the adrenalin seeped away from his organs, Francis felt pleased to learn that the quill had not been pulverized for some hedgerow fertilizer.

"What does it want?" asked Rochalle from within Francis' arm, where she had sought safety.

"I think it wants some remuneration."

"Give him a sovereign and bid him leave us."

"I shall." As Francis approached the quill, he saw by the absence of the small tusks and the pods on its back that it was a female quill. Well, after all, female or not, Francis remembered Bradley-Cooper had said they were completely democratic and that must extend to manual labor as well. He reached out his hand with the gold coin. Swiftly the she-quill took his hand and brought it up to her snout where she rubbed it across the lump there. Her grip was firm but gentle. After the initial shock had faded, Francis stood stock-still. His hand tingled from the contact with the quill's sensitive zone. Just as quickly the she-quill released his hand and deftly turned out of the stateroom door.

"What was that all about?" asked Rochalle, her feminine instincts well machined to the point they told her that some other female had made advances toward her mate.

"I really don't know. That quill was expressing something— its gratitude." A shiver ran up his spine. "Never mind, a minor incident. Come now, girl, we have much unpacking to do, the trip of a week lies ahead of us, the open sea, the salt breezes, perhaps even an electrical storm. The ship's captain said it was the season; they're quite dramatic. You've never seen one?"

"No," she said, not quite satisfied by Francis' explanation of the bizarre actions of the quill. Soon, however, she was busily rearranging their clothing, ordering dinner, and bathing her hair while Francis settled down in a lounge chair outside on their private deck and closed his eyes with a long sigh.

Wind-swept foam highlighted the afterdeck as canisters of flamicide exploded upward, arching over the stern of the ship, to break up the sargasso accumulation of the sea quill, which, propelled by their umbrella-like flippers, clogged the sea lane.

Francis leaned on the brass railing, roped off as a viewing platform for dignitaries of state, while below him the mammoth herd of sea quill tossed and turned lazily, whipping the calm seas up to sooty-brown froth.

"It's a good opportunity to empty our bilges. The kitchen helpers shake the refuse barrels now," said the ship's captain who had come along the railing, polishing it with his white gloves.

"Why so?" asked Francis.

"Great garbage eaters, the sea quill; much like their brethren on terra firma."

The metal cans were emptied over the railing below them from the galley level. Like gold doubloons the pieces brought the sea quill to diving and splashing about with much fanfare. As their great silky bulks turned in the waves, their musical calls went out to one another in an ever-undulating chorus of sound.

It had seemed an eternity before the canisters impacted the great herd. The deep-seated thud of the exploding containers was soon followed by geysers of sky-flung water, flaming red. In an instant the entire congregation of thousands of sea quill disappeared beneath the waters, grim with the remains of the unlucky. The sea went smooth as glass. With the calm, the breeze had faltered away and Francis found that he himself held his own breath. The boundless heave of the sea waters became unresisting once more, a blot of color on the red-stained horizon.

"We won't see them again for a while," said the captain. He signaled the men away from the firing stands.

The ship went on unimpeded, trampling down the small swells and wavelets that broke halfheartedly on the bowsprit. Francis felt the cunning beneath the waves. Like torpedoes, thoughts split along the surface of his mind. He equated the so-many-tons of quill blubber and bones with his wire-strung skeleton. For a wild moment, he wanted to fling himself headlong into the beckoning sea. Struck between the shoulder blades by the padded hand of the captain, Francis found himself once more aboard a ship sailing for the mythical dreamland of Innisfree.

"Don't let the sea depress you, Sir Francis, it would drag you down fifty fathoms if it could. A million men lie wrapped there in those invisible tentacles. Come, join us in the main saloon; we have music and dancing to warm away the cold spray."

"In a moment, Captain, I wish to remain here a short while longer."

"Do hurry. I believe charades are to begin shortly and your lady is anxious for your return."

"Give my message to her; tell her I weigh my thoughts."

"As you wish, but thoughts at open sea have the propensity of becoming lead weights. Don't lean too heavily over the rail." He laughed.

Francis did not know how long he had been leaning against the rail when Rochalle touched his arm. Night had sent the moon to the mouth of its lair. "What is troubling you, Francis? You tarry long from the sup, the food has grown cold. It is too bleak out here, you will catch a melancholy from sad luna."

"A song ripples through me."

"What is this song?"

"I cannot name it, only a line or two courses back and forth across my thoughts.

" 'Brightly shone the moon that night though the frost was cruel.' Do you know it?" he asked. "It must be an ancient tune."

"The tapes have record of it." She thought for a moment. "Good King . . . Wenceslaus, that is it. It was sung during a celebration that was called Christmas.

" 'Brightly shone the moon that night though the frost was cruel.' "

"Yes, a bright moon. See how it sparkles the sea to diamonds."

"But no frost, Francis, no cruel frost is there."

"The frost is in my heart and it is cruel." He turned away and walked off in the darkness.

Q

"I knew you would be up late," she said, "that is why I lay awake till now."

"I am a shipwreck," said Francis, as if exhausted to the core. "A scuttled hulk, I desert my own ship."

"What is this despair you fall victim to? I do not understand. You have everything, why are you not happy?"

"Happy? I was happier as an assassin. At least I knew everything for what it was, clear and simple. I killed or I was killed. When the man I sought died, he stayed dead; he did not come back to plague me with doubts. I was loathsome and scumlike but I lived my own life, hated myself freely, could hold my scum in my own two fists. Now some malignancy has given me reason and hope and a sham of confidence. I am not my own man any longer. I might just as well turn myself in for a bright new Automatic."

Rochalle's green eyes fell heavily.

Francis took her into his arms. "I did not mean you, Rochalle. The only care I have to continue rests with you; never doubt that."

"I do not doubt. It was selfish of me to feel offended. Come lie with me," she said.

He blew out the candle and made his way into her. The world sank away with the setting moon beneath the lapping serenity of the dispassionate sea. Francis freed himself from the despoiled toy-day torn by the burnt bodies of the childlike quill. He freed himself from the heavy-shouldered feeling that had weighed upon him these past days aboard ship. It must have been caused by the monotony of endless waves and gray-washed skies, this premonition of catastrophe and doom. Outside, a deaf-mute electrical storm frustrated itself in the dark clouds.

Q

He awoke the next morning to the news that a flotilla of small craft from Innisfree had come out to meet them since it now was only a day's cruise from port. There was to be a gala dinner party for the passengers. Although no official envoy seemed to be among the sun-tanned faces of the small pleasure-craft, aglow with colored lights and trailing brightly embroidered flags and sails, Rochalle hurried about helping the crew to prepare the night's festivities, organizing, inviting all the passengers personally, tasting the pies and gravy in the kitchen, while Francis spent the afternoon preparing his speech of greeting to the council and people of Innisfree. After the previous months' experience, during which he had been called upon to write more and more of the Baron's open letters to the people, he had gained considerable skill and adroitness with the written word as well as with diplomatic procedure. He sat in the small study off the sleeping quarters in a silk robe given to him by one of the boatsmen from Innisfree. It was woven with that strong yet supple material indigenous to that land and was richly decorated with hand-embroidered signs and symbols, all unintelligible but curiously pleasing to Francis.

A gentle calm had spread over the water as the ship came closer to the shore, the smaller boats were carried by the wake of the ship like raindrops on glass. He could smell the sweetmeats, which were being arranged on the silver serving trays, and hear the hubbub of busy voices moving over the deck as streamers and lights were hung. The words of his initial address flowed like the billowing sleeves of the new robe in an easy stream of words. "People of Innisfree, I bear with me the citation of the Baron of Brentwood, of Leicester, Bath, and Sussex, and of the territories Quill and Montagne. I am bid by my Baron to extend his warmest feelings and prayerful hopes that the governments and peoples of our two disparate lands may find a kindred spirit common to both dominions. I am my land's first ambassador to your fair Isle of Innisfree, in the first mutual exchange in countless generations. May the new era of peace and harmony, of unity and comradeship, fill our hearts and minds with the common goal of brotherhood and progress. Thank you for your thoughtful and generous reception."

It was short as all initial speeches were, but his brief case held many documents and papers concerning all phases of interchange between the two empires. He must be very careful.

Innisfree did not care for the term "empire" nor for secret pacts, it seemed. Francis considered himself to be entering into the negotiations with a clear and unprejudiced mind, ready and willing to give the Innisfree people the benefit of the doubt, although his trained instincts brought him to firm caution. He would reserve judgment until he had seen much more of these smiling faces and their disarming laughter.

Rochalle entered the room calling out, "The sun has set, the lamps have been lit, and you still lounge, Francis. How can you be so composed? I'm almost perspiring from all the activity swirling about us. Are you coming? Here, let me help you dress. I think this cravat is the better, don't you agree? Good. Now I'll run your bath for you and . . ."

Francis sighed and put down his notations, admiring Rochalle's rapidly moving lips. He became even more relaxed in the warm tub as Rochalle hummed a soft tune and scrubbed his back.

Q

Suspended in the warmth of the water, the muscles in his neck and back kneaded and unknotted, Francis let himself drift away. Seascapes and the sea broiling with the aquatic quill superimposed and dissolved over fleeting images of Rochalle and himself walking along bustling stalls of flower vendors on some street with white buildings scalloped in yellow. Someone was talking to him, walking by his side, speaking directly into his ear.

"These flower mongers," said the voice with disdain. "Garbage-truck cardholders that take a lease on the goodness of the beautiful flower gardens, take them, wreck them, sail them bonny blue in the bread sky."

Francis heard himself try to quiet the querulous man. "To tell o' the truth, Markweather, I find this all very pleasant and the people even more so, these people of Innisfree."

Something was patting his eyes. A towel in Rochalle's hand,

wiped the water from his face. The towel dabbing at his eyelids, dispelled the dream.

"I was dreaming of Markweather. You and I and he were walking in a market place of flowers, all the while he was disparaging the people about us. Typical of a security man, but his voice was so bitter, so filled with hatred."

"Markweather seems of an uneven temperament to me," said Rochalle as she dried his body with the hand dryer.

Francis shook off the feeling that the short dream had been a prelude to a larger dream. He dressed and escorted Rochalle to the captain's table just as the musicians began their performance. The bandmaster stepped to the front of the stage.

"Ladies and gentlemen, Captain and guests. Tonight, we have the much distinguished Sir Francis of North Dunnetowne, Ambassador to Innisfree, who is on his maiden voyage to us, on a mission to draw our lands together in a common bond of understanding. The band members and I have arranged a special piece of music for this very special event. As part of the Baron's Cross-cultural Program we have been commissioned to produce tapes of a very special nature. Within the category of Primitive Art we have used our synthesizers to reproduce the music of the quill."

There was a murmur of voices from the audience.

"At first the music may sound, to say the least, unusual, but we feel it has much merit as musical expression. So, without further ado, I'll strike up the band."

From the ten-console band, the electrical hum of the synthesizers vibrated the room. With a downbeat of his glowing baton in the darkened room, the director began his arrangement of "Quill for Ten Synthesizers."

Intertwining and swirling, undulating and resonant, the strange music filled the room with waves and crags, with deserts and cold vacuum, with fire and ice.

"Mysterious." "Haunting." "Delightful." "It will never sell." "I like it." The comments were as varied as the music.

"Incomprehensible gibberish," said the security agent Markweather, assigned to Francis' entourage.

Francis was transfixed. He heard the voices of the sea quill rolling in the surf, the eerie yet delicate mating music he had heard while in the rebel's camp. The band had made skillful use of the themes exhibiting all the subtle nuances and fine tone shadings found within the long wails and sighs of the quill. Even to the square of cytoplasm, Rochalle's only living remnant implanted in his brain, the vibrations filled his being. The embedded life literally dazzled with energy. But the music had a quality of deep sadness, of longing, as if something were reaching out to him from across the stars.

When the piece was finished there was much applause, the director had his players bow before their consoles while the hors d'oeuvres were removed to make room for the main course. The announcement was made that there would be a slight delay with the dessert, which was to have been crepes suzette, because, it seems, said the director, one of the kitchen quill had drunk all fifteen decanters of brandy . . . and eaten the bottles, too. Everyone laughed in good cheer and were quick to ask of the quill's health, which they very thankfully learned was quite well, no harmful aftereffects, at least until the following morning.

"All this business of reconciling the quill with the rest of the population is all well and good," said Markweather, pulling at his left ear lobe as he was wont, "but as for giving them jobs of responsibility . . . well, you see what happened. I say, certainly hire them, give them jobs, if they demonstrate an ability for the work, and not just hand them a job on a silver platter."

Francis quickly asked Rochalle to the dance floor where an impassioned florále, a favorite of the Innisfree people was being played. Her long violet skirt hovering about, Rochalle shone through the sheer garment, her long fingers and arms responding to the crystalline music, with many twists and spiraling turns. When the music slowed to a more conservative, almost somber favorite of the Baron's, Francis spoke into Rochalle's ear as they moved about the floor in the slow, formal fashion of the ponderous music. Her airy clothing settled about her and clung almost invisibly.

"All the women here are mad with jealousy of you, Rochalle. I really don't know if this is good for the diplomatic arena. If you anger the wives, then they shall vent themselves upon their husbands, who, in turn, will direct their animosities toward me. Perhaps something more demure and less . . . less attractive might have been a wiser choice."

"At the time I chose my body I was thinking only of you. I did not intentionally wish to inflame anyone . . . except you, my darling."

"I see. I see."

"Perhaps," she said, "all the men are mad with envy of you. After all, I belong to you, and you display me about. You could always keep me cloistered away or instruct me in the art of self-effacement."

"Let us let it remain as it is. If we engender envy and jealousy, they suffer, not we. It is in their minds."

"And, dear Francis, I do not think those feelings will continue once they come to know us more intimately."

"Yes, you're right. No more talk about this. I think I'll request another floróle. The Baron's music sounds like rusty dungeon doors."

"Look there, Francis. Markweather in the corner, grimacing and groaning at what I'm sure he considers wasteful frivolity."

"No, he doesn't approve at all, I'm afraid."

"And he is so young and not unpleasant of feature."

"What he needs is one of those Innisfree maidens to turn his frown into a smile. Or perhaps someone should stand him on his head."

"You find the maidens of Innisfree appealing, Francis?"

"On an aesthetic level, my dear, of course. Naturally, the cultural differences would make it highly unlikely that I would be more interested than on anything but an appreciative level. I think they are too naïve and idyllic for my tastes. Remember, I am still very much the rogue and vagabond."

"I think you would like to think so, but you manifest strong indications to the other end of the scale."

"From half-penny killer to ambassador in one fell swoop. My head still spins."

"You've worked hard for years for your position."

"Certainly not deliberately. I never aimed for anything higher than a day's life at a time. All this is merely a by-product."

"However you wish to describe it, you could never convince me of your own evaluation of yourself. And, if your head spins, review the Baron. His turnabout may yet cause the Earth's poles to exchange north for south. It is a time of rapid changes, reversals, and surprises. And tomorrow morning we sail into Port Innisfree to meet whatever exotics of Fate may be there waiting."

"And I, Francis of North Dunnetowne, am to bring about, in a week's time, an alliance between two lands who have been at war with one another for two thousand years."

"Yes, you, Sir Francis. You will bring it about and you will go on being uncertain, go on reluctantly, but always will you go on. The momentum of your will shall carry you through history's paper walls."

The plaintive cry of a sea bird drew their attention as they danced in the starry night on the open deck.

"A bird, Francis. A free-flying bird that lives on the winds."

"It is a marvelous sight, how it soars and floats so effortlessly. It is the first I've seen."

"It is a sign. We are close to land. Innisfree sends out a messenger."

"It is said there are many flowers on Innisfree, many birds and small creatures abound. Vegetation grows from which food can be merely plucked and eaten. It is like a dream one has as a child, a dream of Early Earth."

"Yes, a dream."

"Take me inside, Francis. It grows cool and a good night's sleep will serve you in good stead for the morrow. I will ease you to sleep with song, for I feel your apprehension and doubt. Come, and I will sing a quill lullaby I've learned. It brings pure sleep and sunlight in the morning."

"I feel as if I pass from under a dark shadow the farther I

travel from the Baron's dominion. I come out into the sunshine as Innisfree draws near. Yes, let us retire."

They slipped away from the party-goers, tiptoeing past the sleeping security guard, and closed their door behind them softly.

Q

In the morning, the skyscraping spikes and towers of the Baron's city were nowhere to be seen in Innisfree. Francis scanned the panorama of gentle, curving architecture with great appreciation. None of his land's burnt bleakness marred the soft landscape of low, rounded buildings. Bubblelike, multifaceted domes dotted the land in a seemingly random and wholly pleasing fashion. There were no tall buildings, instead an amazing abundance of flowers and shrubs blossomed among the lawns of green grass.

"Synthetic reproductions," snarled Markweather, who sat next to Francis in the open touring vehicle. "A model city, fabricated for our benefit; the rest of the land lies in ruin and despair. Don't be taken in by their guile."

"A point well taken, Markweather," said Francis. His eyes could not move fast enough to take in all the wondrous sights: brightly plumed birds; fawn-colored animals with long graceful limbs; pools of clear water; natural waterfalls of bubbling beauty. And the people of Innisfree, attired in their gaily decorated robes; their smiles and faces so radiant with health and cheer. The sunlight. The bright, warm, clean sunlight spreading across the land.

How could it all be? He marveled that Innisfree was spared the blight that made his land a desecrated graveyard.

The cavalcade of vehicles, bicycles, carts, children on ponyback wound its way through the main streets of Innisfree. At least Francis presumed they were main streets, although it would be difficult to distinguish between the center of the "city" and its outer portions. No building, no equestrian statue, no fortress was there for a landmark. Francis could see Markweather's anxiety over the route they took; he could not apply any logic or formulate any plans without the routine reference points. He was disoriented and it showed in his nervous hands on the armrest. Markweather had donned a rather prosaic mask, drab and rumpled, that was supposed to make him inconspicuous. Innocuous? thought Francis. No, the security man did carry a dagger and a strangling wire.

"Where is the pomp and ceremony?" asked Markweather. "The salute of arms, the band of musicians, crowds lining the streets shouting their greeting? What have they given us? Flower carts and children riding ponies. How dare they slight us with their nonchalance?"

"Calm yourself, my young friend. Remember that this is another land, another way of life. Sit back and enjoy the view."

"But, sir—"

"Sit back, Markweather, let loose of your dagger. I fear those children would make poor assassins."

The vehicles reached one of the domed structures and stopped. Francis' own driver had to open the door while the children dismounted and began to run and play in the small courtyard adjoining the building. When no delegation appeared, Markweather could no longer restrain himself; he accosted one of the cart drivers who merely shook his head under the security man's barrage of questions. Francis and Rochalle were examining the tiles that covered the surface of the dome when the heated and red-faced Markweather approached them with much waving of arms and gesticulations, referring to the outrageous treatment being afforded them by the Innisfree government.

"Come, look here. Look at the hand-painted tile decorating this structure," called Francis.

"I am not a tourist," retorted Markweather.

"Look here," said Francis, with more command in his voice.

Slowly Markweather's eyes saw what he was seeing. The glossy, finely painted tiles, numbering in the hundreds, were all depictions of the emissaries from the Dominion: Francis, Rochalle, Markweather, even the driver of the vehicle they brought and the manservant and the maidservant attending the ambassador and his consort.

"What is this?"

"This, Markweather, is our reception committee. They have erected this for our benefit, painted our faces a hundred times each, made us a monument in their own country."

"It is magnificent," said Rochalle. "And all the different expressions on our faces. How could they know each of us so well?"

Markweather realized the paintings reflected more than their faces; the portraits of him all showed irritation or scowls of frustration as they shimmered in the sunlight.

Softly, almost imperceptibly, music began emanating from the dome. Music that complemented the blue sky and the smiling children running and laughing about the somber-faced Markweather. The music seemed to everyone to fall upon them like a summer shower. Furrowed brows and lines of perplexity melted away from Markweather's forehead. Francis and Rochalle saw the transformation as some of the children took Markweather by the sleeves of his robe and brought him to one of the golden ponies. Before he knew it, he was mounted and being led through the streets by the smiling children who hummed the same wondrous melody. Throngs of naked children flowed into the streets and skipped merrily behind Markweather as he piloted the pony through the city.

Only Francis and Rochalle saw the changes. The painted tiles which bore the faces of Markweather lost their unhappy cast and took on new and lighter auras. They put their arms around one another and marveled in thankfulness at the dream come true all about them.

The days passed, although no one counted them; it could have been a week, a day, a single morning. Everyone rambled about or played with the children or frolicked in the streams or listened to the music domes or admired the art domes. No committee ever appeared; no delegation; no king or king's emissary. The people of Innisfree exchanged greetings with them as they passed about their business, gave them food and drink. There were never any panel meetings or council chambers or signing of parchments. There was no thought amongst them, not even Markweather, who had become the children's hero with his war whoops and the games he invented. Rochalle and Francis' bond mellowed deeper every moment they lay under the deep amber sun. There was not a thought among them about the place of their departure, for that was all that the Baron's Dominion, their homeland, had become. Not a thought until the gunship's rotary blades chopped up the spangled sunset with its harsh search beam and metallic loudspeaker peppering the languid bodies lying on the green lawns.

"Sir Francis of North Dunnetowne. Sir Francis of North Dunnetowne, identify yourself."

Francis stood up squinting into the glaring light.

The gunship maneuvered in for a landing. As it touched down, the streets became deserted. The music stopped; the laughter died away.

Markweather in confounded rage at the intrusion of the monstrosity in his newfound paradise, ran toward it, shaking his fist, and yelling above the noise.

"Get out, get out. You can't do this; you're violating sovereign airspace. . . ."

He stopped shouting. He realized how silly his protest was, "violating airspace." Innisfree guarded no airspace from intrusion; its borders were as open as the doors and windows of its structures. He turned his face away from the prop wash and refused to look at the security guards emerging from the craft.

"Sir Francis, we have come to escort you back to the Citadel. The Baron wishes your prompt and speedy return rather than the week the ocean voyage would require. A mother craft awaits us just off the coast. Please follow me." The sergeant turned and began walking back toward the gunship. When he heard no one following, he turned once more.

"Sir Francis, please hurry. The Baron asks you to attend him in council at the earliest possible hour. The Dominion is on full alert; an uprising of the first magnitude has begun. Did you not hear me? The situation is grave. We cannot linger here another moment."

Francis and Rochalle looked about them for a few seconds longer, said their silent good-bys and followed the officer aboard.

"Markweather," said Francis.

"Who?"

"The security officer, a member of our party."

A spotlight flashed across the darkened field.

"I see no one else; the field is empty. We cannot spare time for a search. He will have to remain here. I am sorry."

The gunship sprang off the field and pivoted sharply westward.

Sorry, said Francis to himself, still numbed by the sudden fracture of events. He stared out through the bomb-bay door and said nothing more. He felt as if he had just abruptly awoken from an afternoon nap. Afternoon naps always left him with a taste of spoilage in his mouth and disoriented anger in his mind.

Q

The Baron came and went like a smoke-filled room. He bent in among the hinges of time, flinging the dust of two thousand years about him as he hammered his words home.

"I cannot overestimate the undaunted belligerency of our enemies. They send, time and again, squads of syphilitic goons to terrorize the hamlets and fledgling communities now just budding with new life. Lest they set our seas to boiling and our tongues to scupper pipes for their own foul use, break their backs on the wheels of our legions. Break their backs lest they tear our walls to shreddy lacerations and bury our bodies in common dung heaps. Bring me their women and their children, bring me their treasures and their gold but do not bring them. Let no one ever see or hear of them again. To the last infidel.

"Hot and heavy, gush or guess, lay them to waste upon the broken fields of the land. Give them no place to bury their dead; cripple their souls with fire thongs and tie their ears on a string necklace about my throat. Tell them that I wear the ears of their dead about my neck!"

Francis knew that the ball had round-wound itself back to its bloody origins. He knelt down inside himself and blew his breath on the cold fingers of fear wiggling madly before his eyes. He tumbled backward into the oven temperatures of the killing wires and death bullets. Old cruelties sucked in their guts and broadened out their shoulders martialed to the Baron's music. "Death to slayers of the farmlands! Death to the jackals of terror! Death to procurers of death!"

Francis felt how easy it was to turn into beast with the prey's blood in range. The men around him brought their voices to loud shouting and chanting for the final destruction of the enemy. Their voices annealed the cups of defeat over his ears so that they echoed like all the seas. He felt the dread mount up his spine and drop to the center of his brain where it congealed and expanded bladderlike with the venom injected by the Baron's words, his very presence, his seven-foot, chromed body armor. Spurts of fire and spark glinted behind the mirror eye slits of the Baron's war mask.

"Mount your gunships and follow the flame of my sword!"

The room emptied itself into the courtyard where the gun crews wrapped the belts of ammunition and warmed up their engines. Francis and a camera crew went aboard the command ship and strapped themselves in while the Baron spoke to a circle of his commanders.

Francis looked about him at all the engines of destruction, the combat-geared men, the braces of foaming sarks, and thought himself in a dream. He looked about him and shook his head. He hadn't even had time to change from his embroidered tunic, the gift from Innisfree.

Up the ship lifted, whirred about in the frozen air for an instant and shot northward, the swarm of armor-finned gunships buzzing at its tail.

Speaking more to himself than anyone, Francis asked the gleaming back of the Baron's head shield, "Who is the enemy?"

No one answered; the film team was busily recording the

flight of fighters rising like bubbles of air from the ground below. The Baron sat rigid and unmoving, almost invisible against the panel light's flicker.

"How will I know the enemy?" Francis said, almost hysterically.

Without turning the brilliant chromed head, the Baron answered, "You put forth that question on our first meeting, I recall. I gave you a singing dagger and told you that it would call out to you the names of the enemy. This day *I* will show you the enemy."

"Who are they? Where are they? Who are their leaders? It could not be the work of Innisfree. . . ."

"Innisfree? Of course not, Sir Francis. Not Innisfree, but a double traitor among us . . . leads the enemy . . . to such infamous successes."

"A traitor?"

"The Captain of my guard."

"But I had thought the Captain stood in charge of the forces quelling the insurrectionists in the mountains. I have not seen of him from the last spring equinox."

"Nor I. It appears that true to his adulterated composition, his half-breed malevolency, the Captain yielded to the call of the mating season and took a woman, whether quill or woman we don't know, and fathered a son who is claimed by their prophets to be the Harbinger foretold by the ancient myths. They give credence to the night of the glowing brain bags when they hovered over his birthplace. This child performs miracles, they say, rends the heavens and the seas. His father has called for a holy war of retribution, foments the quill and the bands of fugitive criminals to reclaim the homeland of the Quill Nation. He has armed them, trained them, regrouped them under his banner. We go now to stave off their concerted invasion before it breaks over the land."

"And the quill that live in our cities and villages, that work in our factories and public places, what of them?"

"It was a problem; how to discern the traitorous quill from the Dominion-loving. They all share the same amorphous appearance. So they were all gathered up and detained for further examination. Of course, those we found in the acts of arson or espionage were immediately referred to the Burning House which has been reactivated during this national emergency."

All over again, thought Francis. He looked down in the dense forests of the Quill Region, pocked every now and then with a burned-out village or glinting scraps of a downed vehicle. He had not spent much time in the air; the land seemed toylike below. Miniature houses and trees like some child's dollhouse furniture sprinkled the ground rushing away beneath them. He had an inclination to jump, to fly, to drift along the currents of air. He felt the restraining grasp of the safety harness and settled back into the couch. Were it not for the cracking voices from the radio, the whirr of the blades would have almost droned him to sleep.

The sound of splintering glass woke Francis to full awareness.

Be calm; merely a test firing of the guns, he told himself.

Francis looked behind and below him where puffs of green-colored explosions dotted the air as the armada fired its weapons into the cloud bank. The clouds evaporated.

"Radio the commanders to cease firing."

The fleet of bristling gunships cruised lower, to just above the treetops, skimming the surface of the forests, their shadows leaping over the boulders and low hills until they reached the ancient nesting ground of the quill.

"Here in these mountains the Captain has his headquarters near Loch Ness. There is a narrow pass through which only one gunship can negotiate at a time. We enter the valley that harbors their camp through it. Order the ships to cut their engines; we glide in from this point."

The Baron's command ship issued forth from the edge of night and floated on the tidal wave of blackness, the flood tide of gunships cresting behind. The engines were cut, the sarks muzzled to silence, the whispering descent began. Hushed, only the red eyes of the sark shone out of the darkened cockpit. The ships settled like leaves onto the meadow, a slight rustle among the night sounds of cricket and wind. The men glided out and lay in the soft grass, their weapons strapped behind their heads. Responding to the hand signals of their leaders they crept over the field in their camouflage uniforms. Their war masks were flat black so as not to reflect betraying light. The sarks crept belly low, muscles taut, shoulders straining behind their teeth fitted with steel points.

Francis sat within the bubble of the command ship with the Baron who strapped on a fire machine, the old cruelty all about him. Francis found himself with a new zephyr, its round cylinders filled with expansion bullets as he followed the Baron. As the scouts reported the encampment just over the ridge of the hill, the Baron cleared the chamber for firing and with a long sweeping stare into the faces of his men grouped around him, he turned without speaking and began mounting the hill; the men followed. Halfway up the hill someone began shouting cries of battle . . . louder and louder, the voices of the troops rose in shouts and yells until, with one concerted burst of sound, they crested the hill and paused, weapons held above their heads, and charged down the hill with the Baron at the lead, the ground shaking under his great weight.

The camp was asleep when the troopers descended upon it, firing and yelling into every hut and tent, every trench and hole dug by the quills for nesting. Every inch of ground was raked with heavy and continuous fire, explosions rocked them, fire burnt them. Half a dozen gunships strafed the surrounding area with bursts of rocket and cannon fire.

Suddenly a star shell lit up the sky over the camp, dripping incandescent light, blinding the troopers. Francis looked away from the flare as he walked aimlessly among the burning debris, firing his weapon every now and then at a flickering flame or smoking ember. He found himself at the center of the encampment with the rest of the men, their faces blackened with smoke, their weapon barrels fire hot, before the figure of the Baron.

"The camp is deserted, evacuated. There are no quill. Return to your ships," declared his voice.

A crashing sound sprang from the thicket behind them, something hurtled out. Francis found himself spinning about, firing from the hip with the precision of his years as assassin. The form fell; the young quill, still with its orange fur and blue eyes, was alive when the troopers reached its twitching body. It tried to raise itself from the ground, but crumpled, fell on its back, eyes rolling upward, looking for the gazing spot of death. The Baron reached down and put his hand weapon between its eyes and fired.

Q

As the gunship streaked homeward, the Baron addressed his troops via the radio.

"And again I thank you; all of you were volunteers. The fact that the enemy had fled does not dim the courage or valor of you troopers. The people of the Dominion will know that our mission, though it did not succeed completely, did cause the enemy to postpone their invasion plans in order to regroup. And, on the positive side, we do have the kill, the kill is credited to Sir Francis of North Dunnetowne. Truly a soldier and an advisor *extraordinaire*."

The soft orange fur of the small quill fluffed by the breeze, the bright blue of its eyes wilting, the whimpering sounds as it tried to crawl into the brush flashed back and forth into Francis' mind. And the Baron cutting off its ears . . .

Liquefied and perennial, the gleams of the snow-capped levees glistened as the contrails of the ships laced the upper airfields. Francis felt an illness in all his organs. Brain bags covered and recovered his head, sucking his soul away. "Peace," he cried out. "Peace."

"What is it you say?" asked the Baron.

Francis turned his eyes away from the mask of the Baron, its neckpiece spotted with crimson blood. "*Coup de grâce*, is that what you are thinking, Sir Francis? That the kill belongs to me because I administered the final shot? You brought it down with the first fire; the kill is yours, there is no dispute. Take the pelt, my collection is overstocked."

Francis shook his head.

"As you wish, but they make fine polishing cloths. Look how it shines my breastplate."

Francis could not look. He did not let himself vomit for he knew that with his war mask on, he would drown in it, choke to death on his own horror and revulsion.

"Repair to the Citadel"—ordered the Baron—"time for food and merriment, Sir Francis. Ambrosia and nectar for all."

Q

Francis bit into the giblet gravy and listened to the uproarious guffawing of the others in the banquet hall as they jostled goblets of dark wine and threw hunks of meat to the sarks which slunk under the long oaken tables. A continual coming and going of food and drink trays wove in among those dancing the tarantella, bitten by the spider of wine. In their twirling and singing, the cacophony of voices clamoring, and musicians too intoxicated to control their instruments, the single sound of Francis' own ear took hold of him. A ringing, an electrical humming, a wavering moan, it started in his right ear and then skipped back and forth through his skull, setting his teeth on edge. He put his hands over his ears but to no avail. There was a throbbing point in his brain. He drank down a full goblet of wine without any diminution of the sound that hung over his senses like a heated moan, a mirage of pain. Then it came to him, the source of the disjointed pain, and the pain ceased. It was the implanted cytoplasm from Rochalle. Earlier when he had tried to use it to signal out Rochalle at the train station, he had not been successful with its use, but now Rochalle had reached him. The din of the banquet hall and the sluggish response of his body from the wine formulated no question or answer. Perhaps, he mused, his fatigue and the drinking had eased him to a point where the communication was now functioning. He left it at that and fell asleep into his dish of haggis, into the peace of a nightmare-free sleep.

"Voodoo." He awoke with the word in his parched mouth.

His eyes opened into the flaming red eyes of a bitch sark tugging at a piece of meat pinned against the table by Francis' numbed arm. The creature took fright and crawled rapidly from the table, dropping off the edge to the floor, then away out of the deserted room.

He thirsted for water, his stomach felt corroded, his eyes rivaled the sark for scarlet. It was early morning, he judged by the feeble light trickling through the windows, stinging his eyes.

The old woman in brown orthopedic shoes and carrying a bucket of steaming soapy water, scratched her nose with the end of the mop handle.

"Can I help you, sir?" she asked.

Francis shook his head and made an effort to stand up from the bench. His arm, numb from his sleeping on it, fell off the table like the escaping sark. He picked it up by his other hand and tucked it into his robe. He walked slowly past the faded cloth of the old woman, the sickly steam rising from her bucket into his face. He staggered for a moment and went on, the retching burst of bubbles popping in his veins. In his chamber's cool quiet he stood before the wall mirror, looking into his face encrusted with the previous night's dinner.

For a long while he lay beneath the cleansing nozzles of the spray screen before letting the sonic blower peel the moisture and germs from his pores. He switched his sleeping platform onto nondisturbance, adjusting the thermostat to his body temperature, and set a peristaltic rhythm of ten slow undulations per minute. Just at the brink of sleep he thought of Rochalle. She must have gone out, but he saw that her sleeping plugs had gone the night unused, her recharger unruffled. Something tugged at his sleeve. He turned his head. It was the face of the old woman, with a sheen of dirty soap over her scruffy face. Something tickled his leg, the long greenish tongue of a sark was licking it. Someone kissed his cheek, the punctured face of the young quill stared into his face. Francis screamed.

He screamed, the nightmare faded. He sat up, chest heaving. The room was still cool, quiet. Responsive strains of a light cantata nestled against him from the headboard speaker. He felt as if some fever had invaded his body and had just vacated it after much abuse. His limbs were swollen, his joints stiff and unyielding, but his mind felt clear.

Where was Rochalle? His body straggled behind his mind as he dressed and planned the day's activities; the meeting with the Baron over Innisfree, a subject still to be discussed. He did not savor the possible repercussions once the Baron learned what had transpired during the mission. Francis decided to suggest further exploratory visits, perhaps some exchange of technicians. And there was the problem about Markweather to be explained. He hurried through his feeding and quickly scanned the teleprompter's summation of the news; "Rebels routed from mountain lair, casualties reported light, end of conflict in sight. Infiltrators hunted in Leister province after destruction of fertilizer factory. Genetic abnormalities up six-tenths of one per cent. Wreck of ancient Chinese submarine found off Canterbury."

Innisfree, cold cuts on the table, bulletproof blouses, the sound of aluminum shuddering, hurtling along the roadway, these flashes bounced off Francis' retinas to calm the storm of bumblebees massing between his eyes. He ran over a reddish lump in the road, remnants of some arboreal creature from the dense woodlands that lined the roadway. The mangled meat became the child quill he had killed; the thump as his vehicle struck the form became the whoosh of his death bullets into the young quill's down-covered body. He told himself to regain control of himself; he had killed many times before. The sentiment over the killing of women and children was fictitious in war. It was a virtue espoused by the paragons of civilization, the archfiends who tsk-tsked wars into being.

He drove the vehicle as he might parade the lingering façade of his all-pervading equanimity before the vestibules of bowing heads and crimson sashes, the chambers of *haute couture* and demitasses, filigree patterns of veins just beneath the skin and reverence for the Baron, the Deliverer, the Grand Patron of the Similitudes.

Where was Rochalle? What caused this heavy weather, the

dropping of the tides to the quick of the shore, the tenseness among the clouds. Impending. Perhaps an explosion of a blimp or a rising of long sunken continents or a massacre of innocents. The weather was ample backdrop for such occurrences, thought Francis, as he stepped across the courtyard filled with humid shadows. As he passed the cubicles occupied by the various state logicians, he heard the interchange of memorandums called out in sonorous electric voices. He was directed to the Office of the Cleanser of Zeroes and waited in the anteroom for a meeting with the Adjudicator. He found himself taking it all very routinely, this meeting with the sinister head of the Internal Security apparatus, for his official life existed now only on a penumbral awareness level. His thoughts were occupied elsewhere for the most part. Rochalle.

Lombard met him at the door to his office and brought him into the triangular room, continually tumbling around a central core which contained a place for two persons; it was said that the only truly private conversations in the Dominion took place in this specially constructed room. Francis took one of the couches as did the heavily bearded Lombard; the spinning of the room increased until all was a blur about them.

"This room," said the Adjudicator, "has been signified the Quotient of Limbo, so named because of its ability to remove us from any physical contact with the phenomenological world. Do you find it pleasant? I do. It reminds one of a porch swing on a summer evening or the moments just preceding sleep on a rainy night. I often come here alone, bring a good film reel . . . sometimes pen and ink to catch a poem inspired by the blissful detachment afforded by this facility."

"Horseman of the second apocalypse."

"What was that, Sir Francis?"

"A momentary image, not worth repeating."

"Yes," said Lombard, gazing about the blur. "It *is* highly evocative of infinite images. Try this easy exercise: Look deeply into the blur and let what words find their way to your tongue come forth. I write some of my most imaginative poetry in that fashion."

Francis felt little difference between the interior of the Quotient of Limbo and what lay exterior to it, but he did as Lombard suggested.

"Lions' tails become fishhooks in the breeze of briny sleet," he said in one expulsive breath.

"Very good, very good, Sir Francis. Are you a man of letters, a dabbler in the art of poesy?"

"Not at all. I merely followed your instructions. As you say, the room is conducive to wild imagery."

"You're too modest, Sir Francis, truly you are. And now, let me try."

Lombard closed his heavy-lidded eyes, his face assumed a quiet composure as the words began to flow. "Oh so how winsome the sails that lie tarry over the land of white cloth and crimson. Sail, sail, sail crimson waves."

Francis' eyes closed under the soporific cadence of Lombard's voice. He spoke, not hearing himself. And Lombard spoke back to him fleetingly, "And for a song and a jokestone . . ." Francis said sharply, "How can you say this . . . these things? My ears are plugged with cork; the bamacles writhe around my ankles. I cannot make merry. War . . . the stores are stoved with billy clubs and gnashing teeth, cunning melodies, calling, 'Way say, way say, way sail.' How? I can go no farther. The sails drop dead at my feet. Fish spring up from the boards and pull their eyes into sleep. Take me to that sleep. The captain calls, calls around the foredeck, but I can go no step further; the boards beneath my feet creak with two thousand years of tread . . . of the dead . . . of the dead . . . of the . . ."

With a sudden hidden movement of his hand Lombard caused the rotation to decrease until Francis found himself staring blankly, asking, "What was the question?"

"No question, Sir Francis, no question," soothed Lombard. "A request, we have a special problem, not to be discussed outside the environs of our little chamber's tête-à-tête."

"And it is . . . ?" asked Francis, rubbing his eyes.

"Our reliable sources inform us that a member . . . rather, a fixture . . . of the cabinet has developed signs of severe emotional instability to the point where he jeopardizes the security of the Dominion. . . ."

"Yes, yes." Francis interrupted with slight annoyance and a headache. "I know the usual incriminations; just tell me who it is and the day of his atonement."

"Pembroke. Tomorrow noon."

"Pembroke, the Foundry Director? I'm not surprised."

"No?"

"No. He has accosted me on several occasions, grabbing my arm madly, mumbling ominous words of warning . . . all very incoherent. Thought himself some oracle of doom, took to the streets preaching, I'm told."

"All very true, sadly true. Truly, truly, truly, no braver man ever served the Dominion, but . . . what can one say . . . the slings and arrows . . ." Lombard sighed.

"If it was merely another assignment, even of this caliber, was all this elaborate security necessary?" asked Francis.

"In our own way we wanted to determine if you had any qualms."

"Qualms? Concerning what?"

"Oh, the use of violence against positions of authority, killing peers and the like."

"Come now, Lombard, don't insult me any longer; you had me mesmerized by your machine. I know when I've been interrogated."

"Forgive me for my naïve approach to a sticky problem."

"You had doubts about my loyalty?"

"Admitted."

"And do they continue?"

"No, Sir Francis, they do not. You manifest nothing more in your imagery than a profound weariness, a well-developed racial symbology. . . ."

"A basic association revolving about the sea," injected Francis.

"Yes, yes, but how . . . ?"

"I have a small home unit. I've treated myself to a great deal of introspection with it."

"I see. Perhaps when we have been of some small service then, inasmuch as we have a hundredfold more wattage in our device."

"It was a pleasing divertisement, Lombard, but in the future, please spare me the elocution of your prolific verse. I find it tedious. Good day."

Thoroughly affronted, Lombard stood stiffly by as Francis left the room. Another frustrated artist, thought Francis, and acknowledged to himself that this man, Lombard, was dangerous.

Q

The Baron brushed aside the report on the mission to Innisfree, even the disappearance and defection, thought Francis, of the security agent, Markweather.

"More important things were pressing," said the Baron, as they entered the darkened viewing room.

"Aerial films taken by the camera crew aboard my command ship during the raid on the quill camp; some very interesting residual benefits have cropped up in the process. As you can see, these conventional films show the terrain, the encampment, even the shadows of our vehicles as they pass over the land; very highly detailed films, fine resolution and so forth, however, not very informative. But observe, Sir Francis . . ."

There was a pause in the film, a moment of blackness before another reel of film was inserted. A purplish-blue light filled the viewing room and threw strange patterns on the screen.

"With this special film, infra-ultraviolet, we have picked up some interesting data. If you look closely you'll see a general outline of the same terrain as in the first film, except a third dimensional factor is added. There, to the right, begins a series of underground bunkers, tunnels, command centers, all quite modern and well equipped, lying twenty feet beneath that rather drab exterior of huts and holes the wily quill would have had us think its camp. So in fact they were there all the time, all the while laughing at us from below in their dens and caves. Next time they will have little to laugh about or with. And, had it not been for you ferreting out that quill cub, we would not have suspected anything. However, we sent a small squad back who searched the area from which the quill emerged; there they discovered signs of a doorway leading beneath the earth. A gunship suitably equipped with special camera apparatus was flown in, filmed the area, and voilà . . . we have a detailed map of the quill underground city. We await only a propitious moment before we return with the final solution in hand. Again, the Dominion's and my personal gratitude for your service. Now look here, this last film clip, filmed by one of our combat photographers. I think you'll rather enjoy it, I have a copy for you."

Francis watched grimly as the screen took him back to the quill's camp. An enterprising cameraman had seen the quill emerge from the underbrush and had filmed the entire passage of events, even up to the amputation of its ears by the Baron's silver-handled dagger. There was his face; Francis saw it in that livid light cast by the flares and searchlights, saw his own face standing over the bullet-riddled corpse of the small creature at his feet.

The film ended, he followed the Baron's towering chrome body to the small audience room. Francis sat down heavily into the large suede chair; the Baron stood facing the balcony doors overlooking the city that fell below the Citadel's battlements.

"You are appalled by the bloodshed, are you not, Sir Francis?" asked the Baron in a voice edged with solemnity.

Francis did not answer.

"I take it that is an affirmative reply."

The Baron's words were low and resonant from behind his state mask of gray and silver lightning streaks. Francis' own mask was numb and colorless.

"There is no need for you to speak; the words echo clearly enough without utterance. You also despair over the disappearance of your consort and the general oscillations of the time from war to peace to war."

Still no answer issued from Francis who sat in deep confusion.

"Insubstance breathes stronger voices, does it not? Forgive my cryptic remarks, Sir Francis, perhaps some hidden microphone will record them and posterity will be better equipped to decipher their import. Enough of this rheumatoid nostalgia, on to the business at hand. Pembroke, for one. Did you receive your instructions from Lombard this afternoon?"

Francis nodded his head.

"Carry out those directives. However, Pembroke has managed to elude our agents, hidden himself away somewhere; you'll have to ferret him out."

Francis thought he almost detected fatigue in the Baron's voice, but attributed it to his own exhaustion.

"The brain bags are aglow over the Quill Region again tonight; Pembroke will have a field day announcing further proof of the divine origin of the Child Harbinger, more followers for the Captain's legions, more retribution for the earth to pay. The Spore Device has wreaked its worst."

The last words of the Baron startled Francis into speech.

"The Spore Device? Has it been employed, sire?"

"Indeed it has, Sir Francis, indeed it has."

"Where, when, what were the casualties?"

The Baron silenced him with a wave of his chromium glove.

"It is everywhere. It was, it is, it will be, and the casualties continue to mount."

"I don't understand, sire."

"Don't frighten yourself, Sir Francis. There will be no catastrophic flood or violent switching of the magnetic poles or a black plague. You may hardly recognize the difference."

"But the Spore Device, I saw it; a small metal case and yet it threatens the entire Dominion."

"The entire world, Sir Francis, broaden your horizons. The entire world it threatens, as you aptly put it, threatens."

"What can be done?"

"I have sent death vehicles over Innisfree and poisoned the seas at Garth. The clouds are mined over Leister and are to be sent out over the planet in the morning with the tide. Pembroke is to be purged along with several hundred petty officials and their families. I have committed all battalions to battle. In a fortnight we meet the full forces of the Captain at their subterranean complex."

"But, sire, Innisfree and the Dominion, the only land masses still afloat; that *is* the entire world. Are we to dismiss all land and life from the face of the earth, return all to the primeval seas, the undivided firmaments? Destroy the world?"

"The world?" said the Baron. "The world? But look, so many more," he said, pointing to the stars. "Come we'll plunder in tether through cosmic gore."

"What?"

"Some lines from a Spore playwright, from before the last millennium."

"The Spore. The Spore. Who are these miscreant gods that they would terrorize my world, waste it, spit it back into oblivion?" said Francis with anger.

"A mighty race, the Spore; they lead a confederation of planets, of whole solar systems unto galaxies themselves. Guardian of a million suns."

"What foul monsters they are to unleash such weapons upon us. Can we do nothing to repel their influence? Surely you, Baron, you can free us from the tyranny of the Spore. I know now that it is not you who directs this evil all about us, but the heavy hand of the Spore upon you, their invisible presence filling our skies with black rainbows, our fields with mass graves."

The Baron laughed. It was a hollow, metallic laugh, terse and abrupt, abruptly ended.

"Perhaps I can do something, Sir Francis. Perhaps you can do something."

"I?"

"Go to the Captain, tell him the Spore device is unleashed, that it reaches its critical mass on St. Agnes's Eve."

"Will it bring peace? Will the Captain call off his attack, negotiate a treaty with us? Will the death ships be recalled?"

"The Captain will understand; he will meet with me. When he does, you must be there to witness the proceedings. I must have your oath that you will attend, no matter the cost. You must be in attendance."

"I do swear. Does this mean we can divert the final destruction?"

"Perhaps, Sir Francis, perhaps. My command ship will drop you close to the Pass from which point you must traverse the way on foot. You will have all that you need. One of our agents will meet you at the camp's perimeter and lead you to the Captain."

"There is an agent in the camp of the quill?"

"Lombard does have his efficient moments."

"I see. Then I am merely to give the message that the critical mass will be reached in a fortnight."

"At midnight precisely," said the Baron.

"At midnight. And then?"

"Wait and see. Either you will accompany him here or he will have you dismembered on the spot. My ship will be ready to leave shortly; you will be briefed on recognition signals and so forth by my man aboard. Farewell, Sir Francis."

"And Rochalle?"

"I know nothing of her, Sir Francis. Remember though that I said let nothing deter you from being present at the confrontation between the Captain and myself."

"I understand."

"Then off with you and give my felicitations to the Captain."

Q

There were moments when he dissolved into the miasma of the 40 per cent celloid artifice worn above his shoulder brace, the neck supporting it on its opaque stock of flesh head—face/middle, color/neutral, so the carton had read. He liked his new sport mask, thought it rather spiffy.

Tramps and steaming boards lay strewn along the boulevard as he walked his thoughts down by the Thames's fog. Some rusted hulls lay interred in the mud and debris along the riverbank walls where the river water had collected in yellow puddles; some bore name plates in tarnished brass denoting their bygone fame; their historic antiquity: 1) H.M.S. *Winston Churchill*, commissioned 1974; 2) H.M.S. *Heath,* sunk 1976; 3) H.M.S. *Londoneri,* scuttled 1989. Part of the river's lower turn was used as a dumping area for anything metal, part of the economy and recycling program. People pulled old motorbikes, refrigerators, respirators, and empty oxygen cylinders, too corroded for use, to the rim of the river wall and plunged them over into the tangled scraps of metal. Some of the tramps had built shanty cities in the larger mounds of wreckage. Some of them were quite artistic, thought Francis, viewing the various shapes and textures of the structures; others were indistinguishable from the confusion of rust and jagged pieces in which they were nurtured.

He liked to walk here, near Hyde Park, in the early morning hours as he weighed his thoughts. It was mostly deserted, this section of the city, frequented only by the vagabonds and an occasional sanitation department vehicle, vacuuming the roads for discarded corpses. The only sound was the bellow of the air horns, which loomed down from the fog-surrounded spirals of the Citadel, announcing the hour and the half hour.

He watched the flickering firelight of one of the derelict campfires, the fleeting figures crossing before it in the dark twists of metal and shadow. On impulse he ventured down from the stone steps to the dry riverbed where one of the men around the fire called out to him, waving from his seat on a doorless refrigerator.

"Come join us for the evening's repast," the smudge-faced man said good-naturedly.

Francis responded. "And what may that be, my good fellow?"

With a wide grin, the man said, "His majesty's finest wharf rat, *au jus.* Sit, here's a plate for you, a bit nicked, and some fine silverware."

Francis took the old penknife and stuck it into the jellified meat dished out from the pot hung over the crackling fire.

"Jaeger's the name, ex-huntsman to the Baron's personal preserve, late of the Royal Guards. Now leader of this merry band of scoundrels you see skulking about here. The meat to your fancy? Try some of this, it may sweeten off the taste."

The wine was poorly made but strong, and Francis was thankful for the hot mouthfuls it afforded him from the leather skin.

The red wine helped to incinerate away the musky taste of the rodent's flesh. Francis felt it burn all the way down.

"A fine wine," said Francis, handing back the flask.

"A good year, 3999. Last week's in fact," said Jaeger appreciatively, as he savored a mouthful swishing around his mouth. He wiped his bristly moustache on his robe sleeve, took out a scraggly cigarette butt, and made motions that he had no match. "Have you a lucifer?" he asked Francis.

"A what?"

"A lucifer, a match."

"Yes, I think I do."

"Thank you, kind sir."

He struck the match on a lump of rusted steel below his elbow and puffed heavily to keep the stub burning.

"We don't ask a man his name or business background here," said Jaeger in between deep drags, "but are you here as an immigrant or tourist? Or were you just taking a morning constitutional and saw our friendly campfire and decided to join us in our noble savage setting so that you might partake of our particular brand of wisdom from which you will better be able to gauge your being and re-relate yourself to the unfathomable Cosmos?"

"No, Jaeger, actually I heard of your fabulous rat specialty and wanted to sample it," answered Francis with a deadpan expression.

"Very good." Jaeger laughed, slapping his knees. "Very good!"

The brown sleeves of his robe fluffed out around his thin forearms as his hands applauded Francis' retort.

Crimson sails tarry over the land, thought Francis, and he saw billowing sails off the seashore of Innisfree and Rochalle's delighted smile at the approach of the naked islanders in their small boats.

Undulating cries wavered suddenly through the still morning darkness. "What was that?" asked Francis. "It wasn't the hour tolling, or the railway?"

"No," said Jaeger, suddenly sobered. "When the air is motionless the cries reach us from the Burning House."

"It's not possible. The Burning House operates beneath the ground."

"Yes, but there are fissures and faults in the earth along the riverbed here and the sounds are carried through and amplified."

"The earth moans beneath my feet," mused Francis.

"Are you a poet, dear friend, a master of the lyre?"

"No poet am I."

"Philosopher?" asked Jaeger.

"Do you see any stone?"

"Yes, a lentil you wear about your neck, it holds heavily down your head," answered Jaeger.

"My thoughts are lead weights, yes, but I am no philosopher." Francis looked the man squarely in the eye. "I am Sir Francis of North Dunnetowne."

"Ah ha, the Baron's High Executioner himself. Come gather around fellows, show obeisance to our honored guest."

Shadowy figures came out of the night like ravens and catbirds clucking and sighing.

"I warn you, I am armed," said Francis, sensing menace.

"We do not seek to harm you, Sir Francis, merely to pay homage, to prostrate ourselves at your feet, to reaffirm our covenant with our Master, the Baron, and you, as his emissary, as his very word, can grant us confession, for naught among us has sinned but mightily; blasphemers, murderers, gluttons, our camp abounds with the seven deadlies most rampant. Would you not cleanse us, free our souls, unblemish our spirits?"

The circle of faceless men tightened their ring about him, genuflecting in the two-fisted salute of loyalty to the Dominion. As they drew closer to the firelight, Francis could see the orange light glinting on their cowl-hidden faces. He drew his weapon from behind his head.

"Come no closer," he warned, his face mask on combat ready.

"But, Sir Francis," persuaded Jaeger, "we merely wish to touch your robes, bathe your feet . . . in our blood."

Jaeger's voice changed, his eyes flamed.

"In our blood. Fire your weapon. Fire it. We'll be upon you before I say Fire!"

Francis fired, but knew his shot went wild. He felt a hand on his mask rip it from its housing; he felt the cold air on his exposed face. Suddenly everything stopped, froze. The group of attackers fell to their knees, covering their faces with their robes. Only Jaeger remained standing, a statue with a face mask filled with shock and alarm.

Francis picked up his mask and refitted it over his face as much stunned as the men about him.

He wandered away, bruised and confused. "What had so frightened his would-be murderers? He would have to ask the Baron for permission to use high-security clearance. He was curious to see his flesh face enough to venture an employment of the Mirror secreted somewhere within the labyrinthine Archives. The edict that had forbidden mirrors, and polished metals, had been complemented by the murky waters, none of which could support a reflection. The last time, thought Francis, as he reached an official transport station, the last time he had seen his flesh face was . . . or was that a dream? He entered the tube and directed it toward his Citadel chamber.

Q

Bright spots of heat tricked his vision into armored vehicles lined column-to-column along the first perimeter wall. So many things to do, he thought: locating Rochalle, the mission to the enemy, the strange request of the Baron, the execution of Pembroke, having a look at his flesh face. He brushed the leaves of the quaking aspen anchored safely outside his private entrance. It had been a costly gift for Rochalle. Now the slightest breeze would set its leaves to trembling. Feeble, a botanist, had been paid to inject it with androgen with some minor success; it weathered the harsh winter.

In his room Francis found that Rochalle had not been there in his absence. He had decided the mission was of the first priority and put down the beseeching mask he was going to don while seeking permission from the Baron to use the State Mirror.

In the courtyard the engines of the gunship sent out tongues of flame. The daydream he had had of tramps and attackers had served its purpose. The moments of dissolution faded; he entered the cockpit.

High over the countryside the trooper briefed Francis on the path he was to follow using a relief map. It was steep and rugged, the pathway through the pass, requiring a steady staff and a pair of good hiking boots which were supplied. He left his head weapon and strangling wire behind in the ship; he had to go unarmed.

"But, are there not wild packs of sarks roaming those hills?" asked Francis.

"Yes, a number of them, but we have created a diversion so that you can pass easily enough. They will be off after the quill we brought along in the cargo hold. We will drop him some distance away and let the sarks get wind of him to draw them off before we set you in."

The quill was brought out, bound and skewered to the doorway, as the gunship hovered a few feet from the ground, then pushed out. It got to its feet and made off into the brush. Soon the shrill calls of the sark pack could be heard in hot pursuit.

"Go!"

Francis jumped to the ground, fingers touching, knees bent, listening, looking, then he was off toward the pass hung in the misty east. He felt the sweet taste of the hunt speed through his veins, his teeth felt sharper, pointed and eager; his body loped close to the ground, weaving through the spiny bushes, muscles meshing smoothly. He almost forgot his mission, so filled with the joy of the wild hunting about him. His hands were clenched, his eyes narrowed, ears acutely strung for sound.

He sensed something lying in wait behind the shattered boulder in front of him. Instinctively, he leaped to the side of the path and lay motionless. He threw a stone to his far right. The response came from behind the boulder in three cricketlike clicks; the identification signal from the agent with whom he was to rendezvous. Francis answered with his clicker and waited for the person to show himself.

A shadow emerged from behind the broken stone, hesitated, and was followed by a booted foot. The boot carnified into a leg, the leg a hip, the hip a trunk, then two arms clawing at the empty air between its shoulders. The headless body fell forward into the dust, scattering its arms and legs.

Francis' body tensed. Whatever had killed the agent had done so just seconds earlier.

Click. Click. Click.

The three clicks were unmistakable; the call sign. Now the killer had it. The clickings began a circling movement, spiraling in toward Francis' position. The insect sound seemed to come from a dozen places all around him. He pulled a sharp stone chip from the dirt and waited.

He smelled them an instant before they fell upon him in number, then he knew no more.

Q

Francis woke up in an empty room, lying on a mat with a bowl of water and a patch of blue light quivering on the ceiling. He felt along his arms and legs to see if there were any major injuries and found everything intact. He felt strangely refreshed and calm, although he felt a small abrasion between his eyes. His face was there; only his hiking boots were missing.

He examined the sandstone walls fashioned in the usual quill style of the pyramid. As his memory served him, the films had shown the entire underground complex to be a series of a concentric design, pyramids within pyramids; the quill themselves having a quasi-pyramidic shape; even the mat upon which he lay was an equilateral triangle.

He was counting himself quite lucky that his head was still in its place when the wall parted and Bradley-Cooper entered. Francis quickly noted the gray streaks in the man's red beard, the deep lines along his nose. Two large quills stood on either side and seemed to Francis to be eying him malevolently.

Francis decided to move first, confront his captors and offset them.

"I come with a special message for the Captain . . . from the Baron, only to be directly communicated to the Captain. I would speak with him at his earliest convenience as the matter is of the utmost importance. I am prepared to converse with him immediately."

"Perhaps," said Bradley-Cooper, "you should not be so anxious to meet the Captain."

"Why so?" said Francis strongly.

"It appears that you have killed his son."

Francis had been led into the room not knowing what torture awaited him. He stood in the center of the slate-gray room lit only by the luminous water that trickled down the faces of its walls. A chair, roughly carved from the natural rock, waited for the Captain. Francis wondered what agony the Captain had contrived; what would be the quill corollary to the Burning House?

The Captain entered; Francis stood stiffly, sweat down his back. In his stone throne the Captain folded his gloved hands and tilted his flat black mask backward as if regarding more closely the figure of Francis in the center of the strange room.

"I understand you have a message for me from the Baron of such urgency it could not wait a moment's delay."

"That is true."

The Captain gestured forward.

Francis' flesh crawled once more with the serpent slide of the Captain's voice coiling through his ears, but he would proceed cautiously, as there had been no mention of the killing.

"The Baron instructed me to say these words: The mass will reach the critical at midnight, on St. Agnes's Eve."

There was a noticeable swaying of the Captain's black armor exoskeleton with the utterance of the words.

"Repeat your message," said the lead-lined voice.

Francis did so and stood for many minutes in the silence that bounced from the glowing walls as the Captain went into catatonic thought. Francis could feel the quills all about him as if they stood just the other side of the walls, the sense of them oozing through as if they were a semipermeable membrane. He could feel their huge round eyes pushing through; moths against a screen.

Suddenly the light dimmed, the water ceased to flow, the room went dark. In the heatless light reflected from the eyeholes of the Captain's mask, Francis saw a silver-fleeced quill go to the far corner of the room where he faced the Captain and Francis who occupied the other two corners of the room.

"Sir Francis of North Dunnetowne, High Executioner to the Baron, the Unspeakable." The words astounded Francis; firstly they issued from the mouth of the ancient quill, secondly the voice was an exact duplication of his own. He was being accused by his own voice.

"You are charged," continued the quill, "with deicide."

Francis was confused; true, he knew that he had killed a quill cub, but what was this talk of god-killing?

"How do you plead?" asked Francis' voice of Francis.

"Nay, not guilty, I killed no god."

"Perhaps," continued his voice from the huge unmoving jaws of the old magician, "this evidence will convince you of your guilt."

In the center of the room a hole appeared in the air; from this hole beams of many-colored light spun out like threads, wrapping themselves into forms and faces just as Francis had witnessed at the quill encampment many months earlier.

The entire panorama of the Baron's gunship raid on the suspected quill camp in the mountains unfolded before his eyes; every face he had seen, every stretch of hillock and tree that he had passed while flying flashed across the floating screen. Francis knew that it was a detail-for-detail rendering of his own experience being played out from his mind like some film reel, activated by the quill sorcerer. Everything from that night came forth, flashing by as from the view of a drowning mind, but the speed slowed down considerably, to the point of slow motion, spotlighting the killing of the young quill by Francis. Even the bullets took slow seconds to glow against the black night to pump small neat holes in the body of the quill which fell like a crumpled snowflake to the ground.

"Proof enough for you?" said his voice from across the room in the opposite corner.

"Proof enough that I killed a quill, but I saw no deity die by my hands."

"To convince you further, we will review the short but joyful history of the martyred god-child, the Harbinger called Quill after his people."

Francis felt something flee from the bruise between his eyes and surmised it to be the control exercised by the quill interrogator over his memory cells. Before him sprang up the life history of the young quill called the Harbinger, the Quill Incarnate. Its birth attended by the portentous display of the clouds of glowing brain bags drifting over his nest; close-ups of the beatific glow of its face, half-human, half-quill in aspect. Close-ups of the Captain, wearied from the nightlong vigil by the nest of the mother. The mother was a quill, after all, so saw Francis; but there was something familiar about the female quill. Then it struck him squarely; it was the same quill which he had seen in the train station and the same quill which had caressed him on the ship bound for Innisfree. But there was no glowing light about her face; the view expanded to the mourning faces of various humans and quills alike on their knees for it was obvious that the mother had died in childbirth. Her body was seen being lifted away, and somehow, somehow, Francis *knew* that her body was later carried to the center of the nesting grounds in the mountains where every quill there partook of a portion of her flesh in some sacred ritual; and Francis felt no abhorrence at the thought, just the over-all feeling that it was a beautiful and respectful thing to have been done, as if it were some vestigial remains of some vanished civilization from some long-dead planet.

It smiled and drooled a little from the corners of its oral cavity. Then the child's eyes turned directly into those of Francis, and Francis felt the difference. He was knocked backward for when his and the child's eyes touched a spiral of energy, a coil generated from the center of the eyes reached out toward him. The child made a cooing sound and seemed to smile directly *into* Francis; the sound was like "suum, suum, suum."

Francis lay gasping on the floor, looking into the child leaning over him from the vision projected into the air.

"Now," came his own voice again, "are you not convinced of the holiness of the Harbinger?"

From a sudden mad impulse to laugh and rebel, Francis blurted out, "NO! But he has nice eyes!"

He shook his head at his own madness and expected some thunderbolt to sear his brain, but none came.

"Then regard further, the proof of your senses."

The film advanced some months forward and showed the child quill levitating over red desert sand; sparks began dripping down from his body to the arid soil from which, upon contact, sprang pools of crystal water, asplash with fish of fabulous color and agility. Scenes followed where the small infant turned the skies white and the stars black; where he flew among the brain bags which did him no harm, rather fell away to make passage for him through their deadly throng; where thousands of quill came forth to the shore of the sea where they were met by great herds of their brothers, the sea quill; and he, the Quill, stretched his body from the water to the dry land and made of himself a bridge upon which the two species of quill joined each other in fraternity and unity.

"Can he pump petrol?" asked Francis, caught up in some frenzied laughter he could not control, rolling on the floor. Inside, his mind was held in stark terror; what would the Captain do after such profane mockery?

The Captain did not stir from his dark corner. The vision faded; the room faded; Francis was left alone screaming and shouting his mirthless laughter through the night, holding his arms to his sides, bound to his body by the strait jacket of his mad howls.

In the morning when the Captain and Bradley-Cooper came upon him lying twisted on the floor, Francis opened his eyes weakly and said, "Guilty."

"Guilty of killing the Harbinger, the Hope of the Mighty Quill Nation?"

"Guilty," responded Francis.

"Guilty of murdering the most pure among us?"

"Guilty."

"Guilty of killing Quill, my son?"

"Guilty."

"No, Sir Francis, *not* guilty, for my son did not die from your bullets. He lives and you shall see him."

Francis fainted.

Q

When Francis regained consciousness he was on a couch, one of three in each respective corner of the triangular room. He on one, then an empty one and on the third, the Harbinger lay in blue effulgent light. Still clothed in the early orange hair-fur but interspersed with golden whorls, the youngling displayed a form more similar to Francis than to his quill brethren. Feet, hands, headstalk, earlobes, yet with the typical quillian eyes, hugely blue. For some reason he could not explain, Francis saw his own couch as the Isle of the Dominion and the couch of Quill as Innisfree and the room above them became the endless sea that covered the globe, admitting to its surface only the two small outcroppings of land, the Dominion and Innisfree. But the third couch, the empty one, for whom did it wait?

"You are curious about the third couch," said his own voice inside his head. Quickly enough, Francis realized that Quill was using the same trick as had the magician earlier, using his voice to communicate. The quills could not talk, they could only think, he concluded.

"No, Sir Francis, we cannot 'talk' in the manner to which you are accustomed, so I borrow your voice. I would have asked permission but I was so anxious to speak with you that I took liberties. . . ."

"It's quite all right, no need to apologize."

"Thank you, Sir Francis. Now to answer your curiosity; the third couch?"

"Yes, the empty couch."

"No, not empty, Sir Francis, for it is truly occupied."

Francis felt that old feeling that had assailed him before, the vague apprehension that something was sitting close by him but beyond his sight.

"Who sits there?" asked Francis.

"My twin brother," replied Quill in the cool, detached version of Francis' own voice. "You are incredulous? As you know, my mother died at my birth. Because of the complexities of the quill spirit and intellect, plus the added factor of the entry of non-quill energy into my making by way of my father, there developed a second embryo which, at the death of my mother, was born along with me, yet invisible to the range of the human eye, only detectable by our other senses, and quills have many more than you would first guess."

"A ghost baby?" said Francis, more to himself than from himself.

"As you would have it phrased, a ghost baby, Sir Francis. He feeds, my brother, as do I, upon the blue light you see about me. He takes a diet of color and light, breathes, sees, feeds, yet his wisdom lies in another dimension; the wandering spirits, the lost souls, those caught in limbo are his people. I see them now as they gather about his couch to adore him, for he brings them their particular salvation—wraithes, phantasms, ectoplasms, phantoms."

Francis looked but could see nothing.

"But I would like to address myself to you. You have come from the Baron in an effort to have my father return with you to forestall the termination of all earthly activities by the Spore Device."

"And you have come to save us all from ourselves, no doubt," interrupted Francis.

"You still doubt the veracity of my being. Nonetheless, I shall go on. My father wishes me to reinstate the Quill Nation upon the land which belonged to their forebears before your people dropped from the skies so many centuries ago. Some of us returned to the seas, others elected to remain in their ancestral homelands, where our nests have been made since the beginning of time, awaiting the fulfillment of the prophecy which foretold of my coming. I can tell you of our history, for I remember clearly my various lives and more, for more than a quill, I, too, have been a bird, a fiery scarlet in the clouds, a bush, a scaly fish in the seas. My body is a vehicle about me, a wardrobe of coverings to be discarded after they have served their purpose."

"And your purpose?" asked Francis, feeling surly and defiant.

"To change the lands into water, the seas into continents, the caves into sunrises, the slag into silver."

"And how will you affect these revolutionary reforms?"

"With spittle. Look at your hand; the lupus is gone, the festering pock removed and was it not by the spit of the quill jaw?"

Francis began to remember.

"By the music of our spheres; you cannot hear it yet, but you will, it is all about and within you."

"Who told you all about this? Who tutored you? Your father? These clichés!"

"How cynical you are, Sir Francis."

"What must one do to be saved? Merely let himself be spat upon by you?"

"Fundamentally."

Francis gripped his temples, shouting, "What is this madness? The Burning House could be no worse."

"Could be no worse," echoed his quill voice.

The words imploded upon themselves and rang ringing until Francis could stand no more; he had to stop the deafening pain reverberating through his body. Torn with pain he reached the couch upon which the Harbinger lay. Francis put his strong hands about Quill's neck, felt the warm fur, and squeezed until his fingers met. Suddenly he felt choked, strangled, as if his own hands had closed about his own windpipe, crushing with his own strength and will. He released his hold and stumbled backward and away from the couch, the smile on Quill's purple lips fading.

He fell to the floor and was once more assailed by the fit of wanton laughter that had left him broken upon the cold stone earlier. He could see the Harbinger float into the air above his couch. Francis had the bizarre impression that the creature was laying an egg by the look over its flesh face.

An egg of blue light with an internal crimson thread fell from beneath the closed eyes of the Harbinger. It fell slowly to the floor as if weightless. When it touched the floor, it bounced gently and broke open. The vibrating incandescent particle pulsed on the floor. Another egg dropped and broke, revealing a second thread which twined itself about the first. Then a shower of eggs fell, releasing dozens of threads which joined with one another. After the final egg had fallen, the center of the room began to glow with the combined light from the strange threadings.

Francis watched them tumble about one another, swimming and broiling into an ever tighter center, finally into one single globe of brilliant light that rose to the very center of the pyramid room and began to expand until it filled the entire room. Francis felt as if he were elsewhere, watching from some other mind. There was a silent explosion and the room seemed filled with some kind of throbbing life; a shape began to emerge as the swelling decreased; a form appeared, pyramidlike, molded from the container of the room, room, room, room. . . .

In a gasp Francis saw what it was; a quill had been born. The room was a birthing room where quill were formed. His hands in seeking death had created life.

The form shrank still smaller and Francis could see details; some similar to the quill anatomy, some more like his own. Two large quill shuffled into the room and carried the fledgling out in a special device.

"It will be taken to the preparation room where it will be more fully developed."

Francis' mind felt as if it were about to shatter.

"Calm yourself, Sir Francis. Don't fancy yourself a father. You had little to do with it at all," came the replica voice. "When you were told that you had not killed me, it was not quite technically true, for you had killed Quill, *a* Harbinger, but just as I have reproduced my own form, I had done so just prior to the assault that took my first form's physical life shell. Now I have made a third because I have sensed that the particular form you see before you now will not survive corporeally much longer. As Harbinger I have the ability to forewarn myself of impending destruction so as to perpetuate my vehicle. Merely a change of clothing. So have no guilt about killing a young quill nor about the events you have just witnessed. But I would suggest that you find yourself some immediate protection or avail yourself of the nearest exit to the surface, for in a very short while your Baron's gunships will begin a major attack upon these structures. I will be dying here, of necessity, but it need not happen to you."

Francis felt the floor tremble with the roar of a thousand heavy gunships and heard the faraway dull thuddings of Cratermakers burrowing into the ground, then igniting, turning stone and earth to magma and liquid fire. The ground began to shake more violently as the intensity of the explosions neared. Leaks appeared in the stone walls and water gushed from them like ruptured arteries. The Harbinger.

The Harbinger rose once more from his couch, his eyes calm and serene. Francis watched as his levitating body took on the form of a huge quill eye, a single eye glowing in the center of the pyramid.

Suddenly the very roof itself was rent by a Cratermaker, its nose cone protruding through the broken stone; Francis knew he had seconds to escape. Somehow he found an open doorway in the wall and climbed the metal rungs; looking back he saw the Supernal Eye, Quill, close. An instant later the bomb exploded, the force of the blast rocketing Francis bodily through the chimneylike vent. He found himself on the ground with bombs bursting in the air all about him. The starlight was early; the twilight's last gleaming helped Francis hail loudly the Baron's flagship.

The Baron's own mirror-bright gauntlet pulled him aboard.

"How goes it, Sir Francis?" asked the Baron as he fired a triple-

throated fire-tong weapon at a group of fleeing quill, each bursting into flame under his deadly fire. Francis fell back against
the doorport, his ears still ringing with concussion from the
explosion.

"The decision was made to attack in advance of schedule,"
said the Baron, firing off a quick, accurate burst, incinerating
three figures.

"Got three of them that time, two large quill and one of those
renegade politicos, probably one of the Captain's underlings."

Francis looked down; below him he could see two large
quill and Bradley-Cooper's smoldering remains.

"The decision was made to attack in advance when our
scouts found the body of our agent and signs of a struggle between you and some quill. What did the Captain have to say?"
asked the Baron, reloading his weapon.

Francis looked down into the sea of fire below him; the flaming bodies of the quill, their fur ignited, ran about, berserk
torches in the dark night. "We hardly had time to become ac-
quainted," mumbled Francis.

"What say? Come again, Sir Francis . . . this infernal noise
. . . Order Wing Four to unload their troopers; I want the Captain alive. Are you stuttering, Sir Francis?"

"I say this is a bloody nightmare!" Francis yelled.

His voice was drowned out by a thunderous explosion accompanied by a luminous green fireball that billowed up from the
center of the quill underground center. And with it, the entire
area collapsed like wet cardboard and fell in upon itself,
smoking.

"Son of a quill," exclaimed the gunship's pilot at the blazing
spectacle.

"Get our troopers out of there!" ordered the Baron. "Bring the
ship around for a better look. What are you saying, Sir Francis?"

To Francis, the Baron's voice was beginning to sound like
his own. The cut-silk edge of the Baron's head stood out clipped
and polished against the fiery backdrop. Francis thought of
pushing him out through the door into the crackling graveyard

consuming the forest below. Strangely, he found the thought made him feel guilty, ashamed.

"Detail the Scythe Group; they know what to do."

The Scythe Group, thought Francis, specially trained at the Burning House.

He saw them, in their smoke-blue coveralls, dismount the troop carrier, their face masks warted with special eye bubbles to protect them from the intense heat. With large hooks in their galvanized hands, the élite troops made their way among the corpses.

Overhead the huge, sealed balloon had been lofted and secured to a fixed position over the Quill Region. The Scythe Group finished hooking the larger remains of the quill and hoisted them into the air where they were tethered and left hanging from the hovering blimp as a reminder and a warning. Their bodies bobbed and dipped in the strong wind, fanning the fires below them, but the hooks held them secure.

Francis watched the pale glow of the blimp fade, the strung forms hanging beneath lost shape as the night closed about them, burying them beyond the hungry eyes of the gunship searchbeams.

He fell into an exhausted sleep on the floor of the ship, oblivious to the burns on his hands, arms and feet.

Q

He woke with a start; Rochalle was calling him. His attention was swiftly channeled to his wounds, already blistering beneath the makeshift bandages and ointments applied by the flight medic.

Francis was taken to the infirmary where a nurse checked his identity statement, after which his wounds were treated. There was much bustle with the arrival of the injured troopers, chiefly burn casualties. Most of the commotion centered about two nurses and an orderly in the admitting room, who were trying to subdue a violently protesting patient. Perhaps a trooper suffering from shock, thought Francis. He could not see who it was from his cot. Someone must have gotten an injection into him, for soon the noise stopped. The limp form of the man, dazed by the strong sedative, was hefted over toward Francis' cot where it was left, secured by straps to the stretcher. Francis could still not see the man's mask since his head lolled away from his own, but by the clothing Francis knew that it was not one of the Baron's men, rather one of the renegade politicals who had joined the quill rebellion. The man's body gaped numerous wounds, burns, some of which still smoldered. It looked as if one arm had been burned away to the elbow . . . the man's head pitched over, facing Francis.

It was Pembroke.

Q

Pembroke smiled strangely. "Sir Francis," he managed weakly.

"Pembroke." Francis acknowledged his presence.

"Your wounds are not great?" said the scorched mask.

"No, some minor burns," said Francis.

"I did not fare so well. The smell of burnt flesh is not appealing. Will I die?"

"I do not know."

"Sooner or later? Is that it? I see. Who was commissioned?"

"I, myself."

"Well, I am honored. To die by hands so skilled . . . at least for me, it would be merciful, but alas for you. . . ."

"What do you mean? Explain yourself."

"As you wish. Is Rochalle well?"

Francis' neck tensed. "Rochalle? Why do you speak of her?"

Pembroke began laughing which quickly turned to a body-racking cough. A nurse came by and administered some medication. The attack subsided. Pembroke licked his lips, took a rasping breath, and said, "You mean, don't you, why do I speak of *them?*"

Francis could feel the seal between his flesh face and mask loosen; Pembroke's words contained a hint of horror. "Rochalle. What of her?"

He bolted from his cot and gripped the singed and tattered lapels of Pembroke's tunic.

"Tell me what you know of Rochalle!"

Pembroke laughed madly.

Francis shook him until the burnt cloth came away in his hands.

"Rochalle," Pembroke laughed, "Rochalle. Alas, I knew *them* well."

"Nurse," shouted Francis. The nurse rushed over, for she recognized the emblem on Francis' mask.

"Bring me salt," said Francis. The nurse looked down at Pembroke and his open wounds.

"Now!" said Francis and she hurried away.

Francis stared down into Pembroke's blackened face mask where it quaked with spittle-flayed laughter. The nurse returned with a large shaker of salt.

"Pembroke," warned Francis' voice, holding the container over the bloody and torn chest.

"All right, Sir Francis, no need for that. If you really wish to know . . ." He laughed.

Francis began to tip the container over.

"The question is? Please repeat, Sir Francis."

"What do you know of my consort, Rochalle?"

"Why she was fitted with a new body by our Foundry some months ago. . . ."

"More recently."

". . . a moment, Sir Francis; I amend my words. A new body was fitted with her. Yes, more accurate that way. And more recently? Why I never saw her again after you brought her to the Foundry steps."

"You lie, Pembroke." Francis let one grain of burning salt drop onto a wound.

Pembroke's face contorted as the tiny firebrand ate into his pain.

"Enough?" asked Francis.

"Enough," gasped Pembroke.

"No more obscure allusions?"

"Lucidity." Pembroke gritted his teeth. "I spoke the truth. I never saw Rochalle after she entered the Foundry."

"How you lie so blatantly; we three were together on many occasions afterward."

"The three of us, true; you, I, and the *facsimile*."

"Facsimile?"

"The Rochalle who emerged from the Foundry was not the same Rochalle that entered."

"Of course, she had a body replacement."

"No. The original Rochalle you never recognized again, although you saw her."

"Go to the truth, Pembroke. Do not pass confusions; do not collect laughter at my expense."

"Rochalle you saw in a vision, a dream; the Holy Depot, the motherbody of Quill the Harbinger. She gave birth to the Great One."

"What is this lunacy you barter off as the truth?"

"Rochalle's consciousness was transposed to the body of a female quill. You saw her at the train station, on board the ship to Innisfree . . . and lastly in the projection of the birth of Quill when her body was shown lifeless after delivering of the child."

Francis' eyes went glassy.

"The Rochalle you call your consort now these past months was a carefully programmed monitoring device; the first and last of its kind."

"Who ordered this done?" asked Francis blandly. "The Baron?"

"No, not the Baron."

"Who then?"

"The order bore the seal of the Secure. My allegiance was sworn; commandments I must obey."

"Lombard gave the order then. The Quotient of Limbo?"

"Yes. Your Rochalle is dead, died joyfully the receptacle of Quill, cheating Lombard of his evil pleasure. Through her Quill lives."

"Rochalle dead. And the . . . the *replacement?*"

"She's about. I know not where. Do you seek vengeance upon her?"

"No, not upon her." Francis unscrewed the top of the salt canister. The nurse admonished him; "He'll keep the whole ward awake all night."

Every now and then Pembroke would break into a long series of "Hail Quill, High Quill," at which time the nurse would lodge a swath of cotton into his mouth. Pembroke was very quiet when the nurse checked on him in the morning.

Q

As Francis wandered about the city and countryside, the ground shot up all around him, green and hackled with thornbushes; it was the lower season and all the rockbrush was in sickle. The sky mustard, yellowed and burned its face into humps of scoriaceous clouds, just back from passing over Innisfree with cargoes of snow and ice. Empty now, riding high in the warm air, the deflated sow teats leaned heavily over Francis' shoulder. Where was he going? He did not know. Where? The wind seemed to echo as it whistled close to the ground where he walked.

The moon had just risen over Brighton, a chilblain in the cold twilight sky. He rubbed his hands, the old wound aching beneath his white knuckles. He made an effort to review things in his mind, and he almost thought he would cry. Be chronological, he ordered himself. He rubbed his hands to keep the chill from rising up his forearms. He could almost make out his face mask in the shininess of his fingernails, so bright were the glare of moon and the gloss of ice crystal. The Mirror. The State Mirror secreted beneath the Citadel; beneath the black corridors the Mirror was kept. There comes a time in a man's life, so it was said and so Francis reminded himself, that a man must be face to face with his face. Face cubed, it was called. Face to the Third.

What of Rochalle? He could barely ask himself that question. Rochalle was gone, destroyed. Was she? Was not whatever, or whoever, the female form he had known the last months become as one with him? Did he indeed even feel anger toward her? No, he didn't. A warmth began to spread from the center of his chest outward as he thought of her. Right then and there, in the center of the desolate landscape, the cold and the night all hanging about him in splendid arches and glittery spirals, Francis sneezed. And with it he had been closest to death, so had the ancient Greeks written. The sneeze cleared his eyes and wetted his decorator moustache. He loved her. Who or whatever she was, impostor, android, salaried strumpet, fig of his imagination, he loved her! He flung out his arms to the star-crested heavens. "I love her!" he affirmed in a loud, exultant voice. The stars seemed to shake; the very Galaxy itself. Something basic had changed in Francis, something turned, welled up, took form. Francis danced and kicked up blue sparks with his metal heels. "Love, love, love," he sang, spinning in circles, arms waving overhead. "Love makes the world go aground," he shouted.

"Love makes the world go *around*," corrected Rochalle who seemed to have materialized out of nowhere to this vast empty plain. He stopped spinning.

"Rochalle."

"Francis."

"Where . . . Why?" stammered Francis as he lurched toward her half filled with desirous love, half with wrathful malice at his betrayal.

"I know, I know," said Rochalle, her long arms wrapped about her shoulders. "So many questions, so few answers. How can you bear the sight of me?"

"I can bear it well. Are you cold?"

"Yes." She nodded.

"Here, take my cape; it will cut the wind."

"Thank you. It is kind of you."

Francis pulled her closer to him, his arm around her. "It doesn't matter," he said after a long silence.

"Any of it? I'm forgiven?" she said, staring deep into his eyeholes.

"You're forgiven," he said. "I love you."

They walked off toward the road and the vehicle. It was no longer Francis; it was no longer Rochalle. They both knew it, felt it, were it. There was no argument, no harsh words, no tears. No apologies, no repentive promises, no demands. Francis took her legs off for the night, polished them tenderly, plugged her electrodes into place, and kissed her off to recharge. Soon he too fell asleep beneath his mask of repose.

The time that followed wasn't. Neither took notice of it in the least. Arm and arm they walked through the rambling country roads, took along a flute and a reel set to compose music and lyrics as they watched sunrise after moonrise after sunrise through the optical filter that made it all possible. Francis did not report in to the department, merely filed a leave-of-absence notice without filling his estimated time of arrival. Left his strangling wire, his clearance card, his Burning House badge.

Rochalle was more beautiful than ever. He watched how her eyes and skin shone, her hair drifting in long streams behind her, as they raced over heather and stumped plain, far from the madness, the crowds, and their previous lives.

As they lay on the sward together, beneath a warm, sallow sun, a strange and delicate thought crept into Rochalle's mind.

"Love," she said, "why don't we make love . . . ?"

Francis smiled, the idea appealing to him greatly. He undid his purple sash and slowly took out his flute.

"Love? I don't think I know it, but if you could hum a few bars. . . ."

"Not a song, a sweeter melody . . . you and I, our bodies conjoined . . . mating. . . .

"You mean . . . grappling . . . like the quill?" said Francis with mild shock tinting his words.

"It was just a thought, Francis," said Rochalle, her eyes falling, "just a strange and delicate thought."

"Well . . . how would we go about it, anyway?" grumbled Francis. "Is this mating more than just love-making . . . ?"

"First, put down your flute, Francis. . . ."

Q

The sun came up and thawed the morning. Upside-down clouds they saw under their open eyes. Francis' mask was covered with rich dew.

"How beautiful," said Rochalle as she traced designs with her finger along his forehead.

Francis lay under his mask, growing concerned over events transpiring back in the City. He had not seen a prompter in days nor had he had any contact with his department. Then there was the small matter of Lombard, for although he had forgiven Rochalle of any duplicity in the death of Rochalle One, he still would deal with Lombard for his part. "There would be nothing more pleasurable for me," he said to Rochalle, "than to return to Innisfree, now that a calm has been restored to the two Isles. The Quill Rebellion has been put down completely, yet this man Lombard still inflames me. He must be put to the fire tong. You understand, don't you . . . ?"

She pinched a blade of grass. "Yes, I understand." Her eyes downcast, wistful at his departure, Francis thought he felt the grass tremble beneath his feet, within her delicate grasp.

Moments like these, suspended in time, stunned Francis with their intensity, as if all creative energy lay just below the surface of some flower-petal thinness, threatening to burst with imminent display. He watched her lying stretched out, legs crossed at the ankles, head tilted toward the blade of grass she had discovered and now pressed between her thumb and forefinger. Her eyes would turn up toward him now and then. Her eyes, he thought, dark gray and blue agate swirls, large and pool-like in their infinite depths. He had an overpowering impulse to devour, to swallow her whole.

"What?" She cocked her head.

Francis shook his head and could say nothing, the words caught in his throat.

"Are you going?"

"Yes."

Her eyes fell back to the blade of grass and he was gone.

Q

Francis entered the main hall, tapped into a wall phone, pushed the locator, and found Lombard beyond the range of the sensors. Most likely that meant he was safely secluded in the security room and within the whirl of the Quotient of Limbo. He decided to wait for his enemy to be in a position less advantageous than his home ground. Francis noticed a number of new face masks going hither and thither through the lofty corridors; apparently a new class of technicians by their robes. A healthy number of females, he saw, younger, too. He noticed that someone was sending in a location query for him and watched the display panel pinpoint him. He pressed the reply button, acknowledging receipt of the message to wait. Whoever it was, Francis did not recognize her from a distance. But she appeared to be one of the new younger laboratory workers. She approached. Very nice . . . but what was that? She wore no mask; he almost looked away. Her face was unclothed.

"Sir Francis?"

He couldn't speak for a moment, then straightened up as befitted his rank.

"I am Sir Francis. And who are you that you are so brazen to go about without a face mask? I could have you severely chastised for this looseness of behavior."

"You must have been gone for a time longer than they told me. Some changes have taken place, rather dramatic I might say, judging by your reaction. It's much the same with the rest of the older . . . the uh, senior members. But if you look closely, you'll see that many of the new graduates prefer to go about unmasked."

Francis focused his eye lenses to individuals and saw that indeed many of them were without face wear.

"Of course none of the cabinet members has chosen to relinquish the old style and I needn't include the Baron himself. Actually, it is only among the younger appointees that the change appears most obvious."

Francis was focusing his left eye more sharply on her cheekbone and felt himself actually blushing behind his own mask.

"Please, excuse me if I was staring, but this is rather a novel experience for me," he said.

"Go on, it's quite all right with me."

"Well, tell me how you protect your eyes and what about the breathing . . . ?"

"Sadly enough, it is only within the climate-controlled buildings that we can go about without face masks."

"I see. So, it hasn't actually reached the streets, this vogue?"

"No, Sir Francis, you won't have to worry about maskless people running amuck in the streets. At least not until we have cleaned up the external environment."

"We?"

"Yes, I am on the protoplanning committee for reshaping the outside. We actually have the backing of the Baron."

"Tell me more."

"What if I told you that in five years you could be swimming in the Channel itself, perhaps even the Thames River?"

"I wouldn't believe you . . . but that was yesterday."

"Still, the Baron is going ahead with his domed-enclosed cities, but now it will be in conjunction with cleaning up the three elements filling spaces between the domes; a patchwork operation that will eventually link all the areas. Land, sea, and sky."

"Ambitious. Idealistic. Feasible?"

"Very. That's my job, to demonstrate the absolute feasibility of the project. Of course we do have some little difficulties."

"Such as?"

"Such as the Baron."

"May I suggest somewhat of a less frivolous portrayal of the Baron . . . for your own sake . . . uh?"

"Marion . . ."

"Marion. After all, considering my position, it would be better if you restrained yourself, at least in my presence."

"Yes, sir." She winked.

He couldn't resist her buoyant charm, her fresh, scrubbed glow, her bare face. Francis smiled and took her arm as they walked leisurely down the hallway.

"What other difficulties?"

"The quill."

"What about them? Are they still giving us trouble?"

"No, you don't understand. The quill are an integral part of our plan. We need them."

"Need the quill? Whatever for? They're terrible workers; all they do is eat."

"And eat and eat and eat, Sir Francis. And what do they eat? Garbage. The land quill eat whatever they can get their claws on, the same for the sea quill. So we have two factors dealt with effectively: the land and the sea. Of course there is a little more to it than the sketch I'm giving. . . ."

"What about the third element . . . ?"

"The air? Right. But that's where we really need the quill. We need them to mediate with the brain bags."

"Good Spore, the brain bags! Now this *is* becoming too bizarre."

"Don't you see, Sir Francis? There are no sky quill, none as far as I know, but the brain bags are there; the only things flying."

"But they only eat that special pollen and an unlucky person every now and then. How do you propose to employ them to the benefit of the environment?"

"It involves a complete retraining program; training the brain bags to like, to enjoy, to hunger for the various pollutants suspended in the atmosphere. And the quill, with their special relationship with the brain bags have a means of negotiating with them."

"How?"

"First of all, somehow they are able to communicate with them: secondly, we've discovered a symbiotic relationship between the quill and the brain bags. I know you'll find this especially hard to believe, Sir Francis, but it involves the . . . the saliva of the quill."

Francis looked at his hand, long healed of the tumor by the quill's spittle.

"You mean," he said, "their spit?"

"Well, to be blunt, yes. Their spit. It has a combined effect of an aphrodisiac and a medicament for the brain bags who live a rather tenuous existence. They love quill spittle."

"What do they do for the quill? What is the other half of this mutually beneficial relationship?"

"From what we can gather, although the information is spotty, the quill have some need for the discarded brain bag shells. When the brain bag senses death coming on, it makes its way to the quill nesting ground and expires there, to be gathered up by the quill. As yet we don't know why, but we have a field team working on it now."

"Very interesting. Now, then, Marion. Of what service can I be to you?"

"We have a very formidable opponent who is trying his best to wreck our hopes. We want you to intercede for us on our behalf."

"And who is it?"

"The Director of the Security Force, a man named Lombard."

"Lombard is it?"

"Do you find it amusing, Sir Francis? Lombard is an evil and warped person intent on maintaining his grip on the world as it is. He knows he could not control a world of light and purity."

"I know this man Lombard. I will speak with him, but I don't know where he is," said Francis.

"I know where he can be located. He's not here. He's away on private business, his evil work."

"Where is he?"

"At the Burning House. Questioning prisoners."

Q

Francis drove his own car down through the center of the town and showed his credentials at the security gate before being admitted to the Burning House Complex. The young lieutenant who had lost his arm to the quill at Francis' last visit to the camp met him in the waiting room.

"Hello, good to see you again, Sir Francis."

"And how are you, Lieutenant?"

"My new arm is working out fine. I want to thank you for getting it requisitioned so quickly for me."

"It was the least I could do."

"What brings you here? Please, sit down."

"Thank you. I have some business with Sir Lombard, and I understand he is here."

"Sir Lombard? I don't remember seeing him enter."

"I have it on very good advice that he is here, interrogating quill prisoners."

"We have no quill prisoners left; there must be some mistake."

"Of the three thousand prisoners, there are none left? All dead."

"Please, Sir Francis, we are not quite that bloodthirsty, I assure you all but a handful were treated and released as part of the general amnesty declared by the Baron."

"Treated . . . ?"

"Well, yes. Our clinicians removed their salivary glands. We've learned that the secretions from these glands are the chemical cause of their erratic outbursts of violence. You might compare it to a minor lobotomy. Of course all surgery was performed adeptly in our own laboratories. There was no pain, all cleanly done."

Francis thought about the delicate balance between the quill and the brain bags. From what Marion had told him the quill could not survive long without the brain bags who would not reciprocate unless they received an amount of quill saliva. He rubbed his hand.

"The only prisoner we have, and technically he's not classified as a member of the quill race, is being held incommunicado."

"And who is that?"

"Why, I thought you knew; it's the traitorous Captain."

"The Captain, but I thought he escaped."

"Not so. However, his offspring, the so-called Harbinger, did manage to elude our troopers. We at first thought we had located his remains in his bunker, but reports have come in to us to the contrary. We have it that he is being nurtured by his followers somewhere in the Cold."

"But nothing can live in the Cold, that floating iceberg of an island."

"It seems that the quill can; we're running some tests with them now under simulated conditions. They seem to stand up quite well to such extremes of temperature as one experiences in the Cold. Eventually we'll have to send some troopers up there; the proper equipment is being fashioned for them now."

"Include me in that party. I want to take part in the expedition."

"Yes, I can understand. You have a special interest in those murderous beasts."

"Yes, a special interest."

"We'll have to have your fittings measured."

"My measurements are on file at the main bank."

"Very good, sir."

"And now if you'll escort me to Sir Lombard . . ."

"I'm afraid I just can't do that now; I've received express orders to admit no one. . . ."

"No one?" said Francis, gently gripping the Lieutenant's new arm.

"But, of course, Sir Francis, how foolish of me. Please, this way."

As they entered the transport station, the lieutenant handed Francis a side arm.

"Part of regulations, Burning House procedure. We do have some dangerous ones under our care."

There was no sense of motion as the elevator descended down into the copper-polished tunnel. Francis felt that queasiness come over him again. That seminauseous feeling he experienced even at the mention of the facility—the Burning House.

"Most of the preparation rooms are empty, as you can see. We're having them hosed out now. Everything does look deserted. Of course this is one of the upper levels of detention, the more hardened lot are housed in lower compartments. But still, thankfully, it's not like the rush we had during the Insurrection; we could hardly keep the operation going. We were still a hundred per day behind schedule when the program was halted. Fortunately we received permission for overtime and caught up. The Baron sent for Sir Lombard to do an efficiency check; he is inhuman. Why he had my troopers working around the clock, even lost two men to the quill."

"What are those carts?"

"Transport to the Burning House. Yes, I know, what are wooden carts doing in such a modern facility? We were forced to requisition them from a meat-processing plant during the busy period. Let's take the tube down to the high-security sector. I think Sir Lombard is questioning his prisoner there. Careful, don't step in it, Sir Francis."

"Thank you. What was that?"

"Something one of the hoses got out. Who knows what, with those quill. . . . Here we go, Sir Francis."

Two guards stood at the doorway. They stood to attention and opened the door. They walked into the viewing room, darkened from within, and observed the proceedings through the two-way glass. Sir Lombard was with the Captain. Also four guards were in the interrogation room.

"It's all right if we talk, this room is sealed for sound as well as for sight. We'll have to wait for a pause, no need to interrupt."

They sat in the comfortable chairs facing the glass as cool drinks were brought in. The lieutenant switched on the microphone and Sir Francis could hear Lombard as he spoke to the Captain strapped into the adjustable medical chair. The Captain wore a prisoner's mask and seemed thin, the veins showing clearly on his clenched fists. Lombard circled the chair while the four guards took up cardinal points around it.

"Captain," he said. "Captain," he whispered. Lombard kept circling the couch, calling the Captain's name over and over again. The Captain looked disjointed, thought Francis. Under the gray muddle of the prison clothing, all lines became amorphous, indistinct. No ankle lumps or knee lumps broke the monotony of the gray lines of the uniform. His gray face mask was blank and unresponsive.

"Where is this Harbinger, this Mighty Quill? You have been persistently mute on the subject, and we, in our turn, have been methodically persistent. Method has its valid points, but then again, so does creativity. We've asked you our questions in a rather orthodox manner, and you have the disproportionate ingratitude to remain silent to our queries. To be quite frank and candid, Captain, we can keep you alive indefinitely and work our little wonders until you answer. I promised the Baron, and you know what that means. I am a man of my word. So you *will* answer."

There came no response from the motionless figure.

"Well, we can wait; we have time. Guards, you may return the Captain to his quarters."

The guards unstrapped the limp form and lifted him from the couch. His head lolled to the side, some liquid leaked from under the mask. The body, when lifted, collapsed as if it were boneless, legs and arms folding into odd shapes. One of the guards lifted a canvas bag and opened it wide; the others stuffed the Captain into the bag and pulled the drawstrings. The last guard slung the bag over his shoulder and left the room. When Francis approached Lombard, he was washing his hands and mopping his brow.

"Why, Sir Francis, a pleasant surprise. It's been quite some time. You must have been busy; I know I myself have been involved these last weeks with our friend, the Captain. Taciturn fellow, not a word from him as to the whereabouts of his little bastard god. But in time, in time, we shall know. . . . Odd that you're here though, first reports had it that you had killed what was then thought to be the child Quill. Certainly all this unpleasantness would have been avoided if that fact had been true. Come, I'll fly you back to the department."

In the gunship, Francis continued to listen to Lombard's account of the search for the Quill.

"We're beginning to hear that great numbers of the ill and malformed have made their way through some underground means to the camp of the Quill, supposedly where they are being cured en masse. His troops are gleaned from all the leper colonies and genetical reservations. I can barely contain myself. Can't you just envision this Quill sitting on a muffet with an endless line of cripples prostrating themselves before him . . . to be healed . . . to be spat upon . . . legions of crutches and stretchers, bleeding gums and wrinkled flesh . . . hours of spitting . . . days, weeks, and the Quill spitting his little heart away on the rabble. I am literally convulsed with laughter."

Francis turned his face out into the darkness so his disgust would be concealed. His hand went to the side arm he had not removed, but he reminded himself to be more prudent, killing the Chief of Security had to be executed with much aplomb. A push from the flying vehicle? No, he had to be elsewhere when Lombard met his fate. Now was not the time. He could feel his hatred for the repugnance sitting beside him simmer. Perhaps a bomb.

Lombard hummed a little ditty, " 'There'll be a high time in the old town tonight.' Take the ship up into that clearing," he ordered the pilot. "Let's see some stars, perhaps Andromeda's milky embrace . . ."

The ship threaded the hole in the thick haze and revealed the clean black veld of the heavens. Even Francis forgot himself for a moment and stared in wonder at the star clusters.

"There's that supernova we've heard so much about lately, sending off fantastic amounts of radio energy. There was some evidence of a planetary system. But of course it matters very little since the light is just reaching us; the explosion came a hundred million years ago. The bright star to the right is the home star of the Spore. Do you see it, Sir Francis?"

Francis was fascinated by the bright globe of the supernova. Light a hundred million years cold. What was light anyway that it could go on when its source had been extinguished for centuries? What gave it cohesion? The star seemed to gain in magnitude as he stared at it. What if all those stars were atoms and the whole universe itself a molecule? If the universe is a molecule, would Time be some organic compound, a bacteria floating in the intestines of some great living creature walking the land of some other planet universe? Lombard's voice jolted him, he telescoped too suddenly back to his self and felt the full impact of his relative size.

"This quill cub, the Harbinger. Tell me more about him. In your briefing you said you saw him rematerialize himself."

"Yes."

"Is there any finite limit to his reproductive abilities? I mean, can we expect any more or less than nine lives?"

"At least."

"You're being very clear, Sir Francis."

"It's the stars."

"Oh, yes, I forgot that you too were a poet. I should let you dwell on them in peace without fiddle-faddling about business. Go on, feast your eyes."

Slowly the clearing clouded over, the stars dimmed and dipped, disappeared behind the thick brown smudge. The gunship landed on the pad and disembarked its passengers. Francis forced himself to shake hands with Lombard before taking his leave.

"What was it you came to see me about, Sir Francis?"

"Oh, something of a personal nature. It will wait."

The two took opposite directions, Francis heading for his chambers and the fresh embrace of Rochalle.

Q

When the official word came that the Captain had died in his prison cell of "self-inflicted injuries," Francis felt a twinge of remorse. The last memory of the once arrogant Captain rendered into a bag of human jelly was superimposed by the image of an individual leading his people on a great movement intended to remake the history of the world. But the Captain had obviously refused to co-operate, thus securing, at least for the near future, the safety of his offspring, the Quill.

Rochalle was packing his equipment when he entered his chamber after the briefing. She looked up and smiled.

"There was a message for you," she said. "I thought you might need these things, so I began packing."

Immediately Francis knew it meant that the expedition to the Cold was to begin.

"Why are you going into the Cold, Francis?"

"We're to seek out the Quill and his followers. There must be some habitable zone somewhere in the Cold, else all those indigent beings flocking to Quill could not survive."

"Shall I pack your dagger and wire?"

"No, this is not a military expedition. Under the amnesty we are still technically at peace with the quill group, so we take advantage of the treaty to open a dialogue with them. All the others will be from the Data Bank, all civilians and technicians."

"Won't the Chief High Executioner be too much of a temptation for them? You would make a profitable ransom."

"True. But, nonetheless, I am going. This madness must cease; perhaps I can do something. Being in the middle of all this so often seems to have acquired for me a mediator status, so I will seek to arbitrate."

"I see. Francis?"

"Yes?"

"Who is Marion?"

"Marion?"

"Yes, she said to tell you she delivered the message personally. Personally?

"Oh, she's one of the new quillogists who first informed me about the planned foray against the quill."

"Foray against the quill? I thought this was a peaceful exploration."

"It is just the jargon of my trade; I meant the same thing."

"Has the Baron consented to your membership?"

"Let us say he acquiesced in that he did not openly refuse my request to accompany them."

"You did speak to him, Francis?"

"Please, Rochalle, I really do think I can handle this."

"I'm sorry, Francis. I just have felt nervous lately. That man Lombard said something to me."

"Lombard!" Francis' face went livid. "What did he say?"

"Something about hypothetical situations, about an assassination and who would take command of the Dominion in the event of the Baron's demise."

"But the Baron can't die. Hasn't almost two thousand years proved anything to anyone?"

"Why are you so agitated, Francis? It was only a hypothetical situation."

"Nothing is fanciful when it concerns Lombard. I think he was indirectly warning you that in the case of a contest between himself and me for the command of the Dominion, he was making certain of the outcome. Don't you see, it was a threat against you to exert pressure upon me."

"I think you are reading too much into all this. Besides it's all premised upon an impossibility, the death of the Baron. And, of course, he cannot die, can he, Francis?"

"No, his Installation was to run indefinitely. The Investiture documents stated that clearly. It is Spore Law."

"Aren't those papers classified?"

"Very much so. I am in contempt by merely quoting their existence."

"The beggar confronted me in the street again, shaking his finger and calling, 'The King must die, the King must die!'"

"He, too, must have read the Papers."

"What?"

"I will tell you something, Rochalle. The King *must* die. That is the ultimate meaning of the Investiture Papers. After the completion of the two-thousand-year reign, the Baron will be supplanted. I was prompted to conceal this information and continue with this misrepresentation as to the immortality of the Baron because it is the very essence of the Dominion's sanity. The one absolute entity, the rock of immovable substance that makes all the other madness seem to be of some relevance, some purpose."

"An immortal tyranny? The source of hope, of meaning?"

"The very premise of our lives here in the Dominion. When all else around us festers, deteriorates, atrophies, when the very skies dribble away, and when the land itself turns maggoty with sludge and slime, what else of permanence is there to tether our lives together than the being of the infinite Baron?"

"Seven feet of polished chrome? Is that my God? I think not."

Behind his mask of love, Francis was pleased with the show of temper from his consort. It was . . . humanlike, he thought. She resumed packing.

"Your cheek colors with anger, dear Rochalle. . . ."

"It's becoming more than I can bear, Francis. Why can't we emigrate to Innisfree? Why must we remain here in this barren place of gloom? Why not the sunlit skies of Innisfree?"

"Because we are here for a higher purpose, a greater glory. . . ."

"*You* are here for a greater glory. I don't want my child to be born into a world contaminated with the dread of the Spore."

"Child? Child? Did you say child, Rochalle?"

"Are you totally unfamiliar with the word, Francis?"

"Why this is more startling a revelation than my disclosure of the Baron's mortality. A child is born! Fiction could be no more strange. I don't know whether to make carnival out of elation or fly you to some distant outpost out of fear. How is this possible? Don't tell me; again it must be attributed to the handiwork of the Foundry and their meticulous duplication of the twentieth-century female. But to actually be capable of spawning . . ."

"Giving birth. . . . The *Quill* spawn, I give birth, Francis."

"Even the words come strangely to my lips. Now I know why you have been so petulant lately, this constant entreaty to leave this sector . . . How much time do we have? I know it must take at least a fortnight. . . ."

"The cycle consumes nine months and I am into my third."

"I see. Well, will it show soon, I mean the swelling and so forth?"

"Not for a few months, but it will be readily apparent."

"But there are so many dangers, Rochalle. Gastroenteritis, leukemia, microencephaly, only to name a few. . . ."

"That was computed for the offspring of fifty generations ago.

It does not apply now, but I would like it to have its first greetings in the world of light and beauty in Innisfree and not here."

"It—why do you call it 'it'? I mean—"

"Because I don't know its gender yet."

"Well, we'll certainly have to find out, obtain some professional help. I can ask one of the quillogists; they certainly have had a good deal of breeding experience. I could inquire at the Embryosis Plant."

"I think it will be a female."

"A—a—gril." Francis beamed.

"That is called a 'girl,' Francis, not a *gril*."

"Yes, of course. Name—name we must have a suitable name for the first child born of flesh in two thousand years. Let me think . . . what about ZaZu? It has a lyrical musicality about it."

"No."

"No, eh? Hand me that book, that book, that parcel on my desk, the one we confiscated from that madman Pembroke. Yes, here it is. I'll thumb through it and call out some names. Choose the one you like. What about this one . . . 'Pizza'. No. What about 'Hamburger'? No. How's this one? Coca-Cola. A name two thousand years old."

"Now 'Coca-Cola' I like."

"Then 'Coca-Cola' it is."

"What book is that?"

"It seems it's some sort of collection of small pamphlets. No author given, but they must be variations on the same theme because they're all entitled the same, *Menu*. Esoteric commentaries, no doubt."

"Coca-Cola."

"Coca-Cola, the first fleshborn. Yes."

Q

Francis hummed the name to himself cheerily as he carried his luggage to the loading ramp. Marion was there going over a check-list and greeted him warmly, thus augmenting Francis' already buoyant spirits.

"Is all going well?" he asked.

"Fine. We're almost finished with the loading, just the refrigerated units to go."

"What are they, those large cylinders?"

"Some experiments to be carried out in cryogenics, deep freezing, you know. Some magnoinferometers, so forth, and so on. We have a whole list of experiments to run. The last team that went to the Cold, why, it was so long ago, they used dog sleds. Our customized gunship, minus the guns, should serve us in good stead; extra fuel cells, rebreathing apparatus, servodefense shields, and air conditioned, too."

"Certainly a far cry from the pioneering adventures of our forebearers."

"A far cry, indeed. Well, I think it's boarding time. Let's find a good viewing couch before the others take them all."

The gunship was heavily loaded but moved swiftly with the additional weight. The ride was smooth and soon the thermal uplifts that caused some minor jostling of the ship faded as they reached the open sea. They flew directly for many hours over the unending waters. Francis watched as the colors of the water deepened from a shallow copper to an intense cobalt blue. Here and there the shards of the continents were thrust up at acute angles, the sediments of centuries clearly visible. Great schools of sea quill sunned themselves on the rocky vestiges, the small shadow of the ship skipping over their huge bulks like a high-flying bird. From the vantage point of the high altitude, Francis could see far beneath the water the pockmarked ocean floor, rent and gouged by bomb craters and fissures. There were none of the rusted cities or ruins of civilization; all had been reclaimed by the silent waters. It was as if none of it had existed, yet Francis knew that just below him great cities had flourished— Paris, Berlin, Budapest. Billions of the planet's inhabitants had lived their lives, but what were they now? Naught but a two-inch sediment of silt. The Spore had blighted the land, rubbed off the crust of history.

Francis gazed up at the sky and watched the jagged and broken moon tumble erratically. It, too, had suffered and now flashed like a lighthouse beacon as it rolled along its crippled orbit. The faint diffuse clouds that denoted the remnants of Jupiter and Saturn glowed without brilliance. The devastated solar system had borne the brunt of the Spore's vengeance. They had laid it literally to waste. Yet the jewel-like earth still glistened under its mantle of water and in some places, where the air was clear and filled with evaporating moisture, dazzling rainbows were clustered. But the Spore was at work again, reflected Francis.

"Beautiful, isn't it?" said Marion leaning over his couch.

"Yes, very."

"Is it true, Sir Francis, what they say about the Spore returning?"

"I fear it is so. The Second Time is coming to a close and it will institute the return of the Spore. The Baron will meet the Landlord and it will all come to the Past. You, I, the Quill, everything and everyone . . . will have come to pass."

"Unless—"

"Unless what, Marion?"

"The Quill will show the way."

"The Quill?"

"I must confess the true nature of this expedition. It has come after many months of work. Everyone of us here has made a covenant not to return to the Dominion. We go to seek the Quill's aid in ridding our planet of the curse of the Spore as dispensed by the Baron. Each one of us is sworn to this cause. You, Sir Francis, were not anticipated. I am afraid there is little you can do to disrupt our plans."

"On the contrary, my dear Marion, my very reason for enlisting on this crusade was to make similar overtures to the Quill."

"So, we are of the same mind, then?"

"Yes."

"How wonderful—then we shall surely succeed."

"Guard your optimism, lest it make you incautious. Although we bear the hope for peace, we are entering the camp of the enemy. Our contemporaries may not feel they need our assistance. If they can truly free the planet from the grip of the Spore, what need have they for the people of the Dominion, no less us?"

"I feel confident. From all we have heard of this Quill, no envy or greed lives within him."

"Yet his father was murdered by us, and we forced him to flee for his own life, butchered thousands of his followers, made the Burning House busy with their agonies."

"Don't worry, Sir Francis, we have made preparations. In fact, we are expected."

"Expected?"

"Yes. We even bring medicines, food, tools, and instruments for the use of the Quill's followers."

"And those cylinders I saw being put aboard?"

"Nitrogen deep refreezers."

"For what use?"

"You see, Sir Francis, the Quill has captured the Spore. We are going to retrieve it. The Spore envoy is in custody."

Q

The Cold lay below them. A dense cloud of vapors and icy gales swirling what lay beneath its cover into oblivion.

"How can we land in this?"

"We follow the beacon. Everything has been arranged; we merely home in on the directive from the camp of the Quill."

Hail struck the craft as it descended through the seemingly impenetrable mists, lightning flashed and lit the gases into eerie shapes. A better part of an hour passed as the descent took them slowly through the stages of repressurization. Even inside the ship, the increased gravitational pull, caused by the electromagnetic fluctuation peculiar to the Cold, was noticeable.

"How many ships have been lost in this region, Sir Francis?"

"Uncounted and unaccountable . . . swallowed up by the dozens. Only the Spore space craft was able to enter and leave unscathed, so it made a natural landing zone for them when they came here. It all seems strange that here where it all began, the

Spore should be captured. But I did not think it could be contained. What is its prison, how is it kept inched?"

"Outside their craft the Spore are just as susceptible as others to the physical laws of the universe and thus its maladies. The Spore was found frozen; somehow it must have left the protective environment of its ship. The Quill found it after he set up his base here and has been protecting it. Through it we hope to find the weaknesses of the Spore so that we may overcome them. The cylinders will enable us to transport it back to our laboratories for examination."

"But I thought you were not returning to the Dominion."

"We are not, but we have alternate laboratories constructed at Innisfree."

"A large organization unfolds. At first, I must admit, I underestimated you."

"As I said, we have been working for many months. Our network includes many thousands of workers from all three societies; the Dominion, Innisfree, and the Quill. Even to the governing of the planet has our confederation planned. When the Third Time comes, it will be the free peoples of our world and not the Spore or the Baron's successor who will guide us."

"And what of the Quill? Does not he have plans for his people to inherit the Earth? Is there not some conflict of interests here, a rather shaky alliance?"

"We shall soon see. We are here."

Francis had not felt the soft touchdown of the ship nor seen the sudden visible change through the viewportals. A small city lay before him, triangular in base as was customary with the Quills, pyramidal in its volume by way of a transparent shield device holding back the subfreezing vapors and winds. Both quill and humans were busily going about, seemingly completely at ease with one another. Francis felt his natural repulsion.

"Come," said Marion, and took his arm.

Francis quickly dialed his mask set to "greeting," arranged his tunic and followed Marion down the gangplank to the solid ground of the quill complex. No one took special notice of them walking through the short intersecting pathways. Francis found the air warm, almost balmy; it reminded him much of the idyllic weather of Innisfree.

An honor guard met them at the end of the ramp to usher them to their quarters and fulfill their needs; a meeting with the Quill was arranged for the morrow. Francis was of a mind to bathe and lay himself to rest beneath the translucent-bell ceiling of his small but comfortable quarters. Just as his breathing had taken on the ascent toward delta stages, Marion shook him awake with her voice.

"Sir Francis. Sir Francis. Oh, were you asleep? I thought you might like to explore the complex with me. There are some very interesting things to see. But, if you're too tired . . ."

Francis sighed and hauled himself out of bed, forgetting his nakedness. By the time he had remembered, he merely shrugged it off. Marion did not seem taken aback, so he dressed and accompanied her out into the bustling community.

"Well, where shall we go first?" asked Francis.

"We could go see the patients at the Dispensary. It houses all the lame and infirm that the Quill will cure."

"Yes, I would like to see some of these so-called incurables, to satisfy my curiosity that it is all not a quackery."

"It's this way."

Q

They found their way to a large rotunda which afforded free passage to and fro as all the buildings did, completely lacking in security, it seemed. Inside, the walls were hung with retractable couches extending in a vortexing spiral to the ceiling. The entire dome could be revolved on any axis to bring a patient to the receiving station where feeding or examination could be conducted. Most, if not all, were in a state of minimal-life function, kept so to reserve their strength until the Quill could reach them. Usually within twenty-four hours a person entering the facility could expect to be treated and released for work in the community.

The meeting with the Quill held very little pomp and even less ceremony. Francis and Marion entered the medium chamber, much like the other modular constructions except none of the hustle and bustle were present; only the Quill and some of his fellows conferring. Francis saw that the Quill had grown much larger and that all of its baby fur had been replaced with a thicker, darker dressing here and there, streaked with silver. The only vestige of his youth lay in the many-colored concentric rings about the globes of his eyes. From a distance he looked no different than the others, perhaps half a hand taller. But as they approached, Francis felt the singular difference, that strange sense of "presence" that emanated from the Quill. Francis remembered the ghost twin and almost looked about for it, then shrugged.

"Sir Francis, Marion." The Quill pivoted and faced them.

"You have come far, braved the Cold. What is it you would have of me?"

Marion could not speak, she was still awestruck. Francis stepped closer.

"We have come to ask of you that you join our cause in the deliverance of the world from the Spore and their agents."

"Are you not one of their agents, Sir Francis, High Executioner to the Baron?"

"I am not . . . but that is irrelevant. If you have any past grievances against me, you can deal with me personally, yet I must ask you to first consider the whole rather than one of its defective parts."

"Please, Sir Francis, I made a poor joke. I know full well of your efforts and I appreciate them immensely. I am glad that you are here."

"Then you will join us?"

The Quill, moving his bulk, chose his words diplomatically. "I believe the question of aligning allegiance need not concern us at this time. We are of the same mind, if not of the body. Marion, have you brought the instruments?"

"I have. We are already setting up the facility. When can we expect to have a look at the Spore?"

"There is a problem."

"A problem?"

"The Spore has been taken."

"How is that possible?"

"We do not know. But we know that a compatriot of Sir Francis was responsible. A Sir Lombard."

"Lombard. You said Lombard? He is here?"

"We know he has not left the Cold. We look for him now."

"Without the Spore—"

"Yes, Marion, we know."

"Can we help?"

"You may search for yourselves."

Q

Out in the rover, Marion and Francis took turns at the periscope, scanning the fogs and frozen mists with infrared eyes. Howls and groans flung themselves against the sides of the vehicle, buffeting it over the frozen tundra. Blue ultraviolet behind the dense mists, the sun was a dwarf star. The special optics disclosed hunchback hills, black pits, and jagged gorges. The treads bit deeply into the frozen soil, leaving teethmarks that glowed with subzero noctiluscent life. The interior of the rover was lit with the dull red of instrumentation.

"Marion," asked Francis, "what do you know of the Spore? This one we search for?"

"We think he was a commander of one of the Spore starships."

"How old was he?"

"How could I possibly know that, Sir Francis?"

"By his color. What color is he?"

"They said he isn't any color. That his skin is transparent."

"That means his exoskeleton is about to shed. He's in the chrysalis stage. We don't have much time. It's about to emerge."

"What do you mean? You seem to know a good deal more about the Spore than the Data Bank."

"I should. I spent a year with the old data banks studying them before they were destroyed."

"What? This is fantastic. Why haven't you ever said anything?"

"On pain of death, I believe is the phrase. It was some time ago, during my last millennial, toward the end of the Spore occupation. Well, you wouldn't remember."

"No, but tell me more about the Spore."

"The Spore/bipedual Cluster III life forms, parasitic to the nth degree. Main food source: A mixture of hydrogen and oxygen molecules. Self-replicating organisms producing eggs; pupae and larval stages following. One Spore, if unmolested during the entirety of its reproductive period, could blanket the earth with its offspring. And it appears that our specimen is about to germinate into an adult capable of reproduction almost immediately. On their home world they limit their own breeding, but when they send out their Envoys, it is for the express purpose of destroying worlds."

"And you think—"

"I have no doubt. From what I can deduce, this Spore is not the chance survivor of an accident. He's been in his dormant state all these centuries, implanted into the Cold's surface until the time had come. It is he that means the end of it all, the coming of final plague. This Spore could kill the world."

"How?"

"Suck it dry, swallow the seas, evaporate the fluid of life. The precious fluids. They feed on oxygen and hydrogen—water; all our life here is of water."

"So we must stop him before he can lay the eggs."

"I fear he has broken free of his cocoon now. With the help of Lombard, that is."

"Lombard? But why should he do such a thing?"

"I think now that Lombard is not here by accident, either. It all begins to clear. Still some questions remain. Why does Lombard fear the Quill so much? Why the persecution of the Quill Nation? And the Baron, the greatest enigma of all. Who or what is the Baron? It all ties in with the disappearance of the land masses, the advent of the Spore Intervention, the Investiture of the Baron by the Spore Landlord, this ceaseless civil and global warfare."

"Truly questions of the Age, Sir Francis. Will they all be answered before the Age ends?"

"If anyone will know, it will be us, Marion."

"Your teeth are blind, Sir Francis." A voice rang out in their earphones.

"What was that?" said Marion.

"I think I know, Marion. Stop this machine. I think we are not alone."

"Ah, right you are, Sir Francis, Maid Marion. Welcome to the Cold. It suits you well, the cherry flush of your cheek. . . . But, business, business. I assume you know who this is by now?"

"Lombard."

"At your service."

"Out with it."

"Bring your vehicle a hundred meters to the left. You'll see my camp. You can pass through the membrane without a qualm. Come to my campfire, and we'll talk. I have something here you'll be interested in seeing. And if you hurry, you can witness the flowering of life itself."

Francis and Marion exchanged glances. The vehicle lurched leftward and Francis smiled. He knew that whatever happened, Lombard would not escape his fate this time. He had no concern over his personal safety, but then, Marion's young, taut face caused him to reconsider for her sake. He proceeded calmly, deliberately, to the shimmering dome of Lombard's campsite, penetrating the screen, halting the rover with a voice command that prepared it for immediate exit.

Lombard met them, hands folded inside the sleeves of his camouflage cloak. He extended his hand toward Francis.

"Turn it off. Turn off your cloak so that we can better see you, Lombard."

"No need for the acrimonious inflection, Sir Francis. Please lower your weapon. You're among—I can't really say friends, perhaps, comrades would be a better description."

"Hardly."

"Nonetheless, Sir Francis, Marion. Come warm yourselves by the heater."

"We're warm enough. You have the Spore?"

"That I do." Lombard smiled.

"Show him to us," demanded Francis.

"First some hot soup and warm conversation."

"Lombard!" shouted Francis angrily.

"But I insist. Then you can see our friend . . . only then. Come sit, Marion. Come sit by me. Oh, I see. Sir Francis, you were always lucky with the women. And poor me, the lonely bard . . . but come, sit, the two of you. I've been here so long and so alone. Our friend has had little to say. I fancy he does not care for me very much, so you are most welcome company. Tell me, how goes the world?"

"The world turns uneasily . . . because of you, Sir Lombard."

"But, my dear Marion, I—I who find himself thrown together with a bizarre set of circumstances, far beyond his ken, how can I endanger the world?"

"You keep the Spore. You hang it over our heads and threaten us with extinction. Oh, why this horrible game?"

"Sir Francis, can you explain this to me? I'm dumfounded that I am held in such suspicion. Please, why all this alarm? Have I said something that has offended?"

"Your very voice is an offense. You know well enough that the Spore is about, or has already left the cocoon you found him in, and is about to breed untold millions of his fellows to feed on the Great Ocean till it is baked and dried to clay. Give him to us so we may learn how to destroy him and the others that will come."

"But they have come already, Sir Francis, the others. See."

Lombard emerged from the folds of his cloak. Sir Francis felt the illness of the Burning House magnified a thousandfold. Marion turned her face away from the pulpy visage that glistened back at her, its feelers twitching and vibrating.

"We are here already, Sir Francis."

"*You*, one of them?!"

"I'm surprised you haven't guessed by now, especially after

your scholarly efforts. We have a way with fleshy disguises. But even the Baron does not know. It will be his undoing. That is my mission, Sir Francis. I'm sorry, I can tell you find all this unpleasant. Let me reassume the form of the humble Lombard. There—the cloak—and now all is pretty again. You can look now, Marion. Please pardon the histrionics. And now, what was it you wanted to see, Sir Francis? Oh, that's right, the Spore. My friend is—uh, undressing, and will be out momentarily."

"I could kill you now, Lombard."

"How dear of you to retain that name. Please, continue. You were saying you could kill me now, but of course you can, but you won't. It would be most unwise. Only I know where the other Spores are rising. All across the Dominion and Innisfree, too. Not many, but enough. I'm afraid there is little you can do about it. After all, it was prophesied, the end of the Age, the cycle complete, so on and so forth."

"Then what's stopping me from killing you for the sheer pleasure of watching you die?"

"Die? Surely, Sir Francis, you must have learned something about us. Death. Why we don't even have any self-preservation instinct, no instincts at all. It's been bred out. I serve only the whole; I have no other drives or motivations or desires. And certainly no fears. Kill me, at your leisure, but then my friend back there will have to kill the girl, and I think that will deter you at least for the moment. Put your weapon down, Sir Francis. Remember the girl will die first. I warn you."

"Lombard, we both know that no one is back there—no other Spore is forming. There are no other Spores anywhere. You are the only one, the Last."

"Quite right," said Lombard, his hand suddenly filled with a death-gun. "If you will be so kind as to drop your weapon, the girl will not die."

"Perhaps you underestimate me, Lombard. Perhaps your death means more to me than the girl's."

"I think not, Sir Francis. I'll take the risk of wagering lives with you. Remember Rochalle. That's better. Now step away from the weapon. Don't be afraid, Marion. A Spore's word is honorable. I will not harm you. Just let me get into my rover and I'll be on my merry way back to the Dominion. I have a pressing engagement there. Now, if you please. Thank you."

Lombard's vehicle soon began rolling toward the wall of the dome bubble which burst as he went through, throwing the freezing winds into the huddled forms of Marion and Francis. The red glow of the heating unit faded.

"What will we do? It's so cold, Sir Francis."

"Get to the vehicle, quickly."

Just then a burst from Lombard's rover ripped open the side of the other vehicle whose computer cried out sharply.

"It's no use. He's destroyed it."

The Cold engulfed them.

Q

The Cold was a fire built between their eyes. There was nothing they could do. The snow, the subzero ice-swept wind caked them with sheet upon sheet of glassy cold. In a few seconds their bodies were frozen statuary. The last sensation to reach Francis' numbed mind was the fading heat of Marion's breast against his cheek as he held her limp form which quickly hardened in his arms.

Like sand the snow drifted over them. Falling asleep, so warm, falling asleep, Francis felt the words slowing, slowing down, coming from some faraway room. Then Rochalle's voice called to him, "Wake, wake, Francis, wake." "No, no, it's warm, I want to sleep. Come back tomorrow."

Rochalle's faint voice was still echoing when the great heat tugged at his face, the harsh odor, the wet stickiness. His head suddenly came alive, one eye opened. Through the kaleidoscope of snow crystals he saw something blue-red, thick, flicking back and forth toward his face. He called an arm to action, to knock it away, but the arm was nowhere to be found. His other eye rolled downward, joining its mate focusing on the form. The left ear first began registering the whining sounds. It all cleared suddenly. It was a sark!

God, thought Francis, he was being eaten alive by a sark, his body too numb to feel it. But that first fear passed as arms pulled at his shoulders and lifted him from the snow embankment that had built up over their bodies. He heard voices.

"The snow insulated them or they would have been dead hours ago. Lucky for us we had the sarks with us."

Francis knew he had been rescued, once more saved from the death sleep. He felt strangely cheated.

"Here, get him onto the stretcher, and we'll sled him back. The sarks will have him at the ship in ten minutes. Quill will probably take care of him personally."

"Who is it?"

"That's Sir Francis of North Dunnetowne."

"What about the other one? Who's she?"

"I don't know who she was."

Francis shook once and passed from consciousness.

Q

Dreams struck Francis about the face, icy blasts of pain and cold. Marion's face, dreamy with sleep, kept calling to him, nuzzling against his cheek. "I'm cold, Francis. I'm so cold."

Francis burst awake, warm sweat trickling into his eyes. He looked around and his head began to swim. Then memory returned in a rush and his eyes fell closed behind. . . . His hands rushed to his face. Horror flooded him. His mask was gone. His flesh face had been laid bare. He took away his fingers and looked at them. Through his shaking fingers he saw positioned at the end of his couch, the Quill.

"You're anxious about your face. Your mask had to be removed so that you could be resuscitated. It's there, on the table."

Francis saw it, grabbed it to his face, and fitted it quickly. His breath held and flowed out in a long sigh after the mask had been replaced.

"You feel better now?"

Francis experimented with his tongue and found his voice hoarse but usable. "Yes, better."

"We are sorry we could not save your friend, the young girl. But she will be recycled."

"Recycled?"

The pain and anger merged inside Francis' grief.

"I thought you could spit on the dead and bring them back to life. Come on, Mighty Quill, drool some on her corpse."

"I understand, Sir Francis, this girl meant much to you."

Francis realized it, too. He realized, too, that his attack on the Quill was uncalled for. He marveled at the great creature's forbearance.

"Sorry."

"No need, Sir Francis."

"Lombard!" Francis' eyes narrowed. "How much longer must I stay here. He must be located and destroyed."

"You are well. You can leave at your pleasure, or you can stay and give us your counsel . . . unless you have more important callings."

"I have a debt to settle."

"With the Spore Lombard?"

"Then you know?"

"We know."

"Have you captured him?"

"We were unable to intercept him before he reached the Dominion. At the moment he is not within our reach."

"But he is within mine."

"Then you go back to the Dominion?"

"Yes. And what of your plans?"

"We build an army."

"To attack the Dominion?"

"Yes, if necessary. If you cannot set the lands free from the Baron and the Spore."

"Then I have a chance? You give me time to make an attempt?"

"A length of time of finite duration, one month. The time before the Spore's incubation period has ended."

"That would make it St. Agnes's Eve."

"Yes. Midnight."

Francis made ready to leave. The huge bulk of the Quill slid toward him, one of its arms offering a small metal cube, highly polished and seamless.

Francis did not step backward but fought his repugnance. "What is this?"

"A Spore Killer. Take. When you have found the Spore breeding ground, set the Cube next to it. It will destroy them."

"Where? What is it?"

"No matter, just rely on its effectiveness. But you can only employ it when you have uncovered the Spore breeding point."

"I understand."

"Good-by, Sir Francis. We have a ship waiting for you. May we meet next to celebrate the liberation of the planet."

Francis nodded and hurried to the gunship hovering in readiness.

Q

The very pace of existence caught up with Francis once more as the ship spun out of the Cold and headed toward the blackened horizon and the Dominion. The ship was empty, he was the only passenger since the other quillogists would still remain behind, even though their leader, Marion, was dead. Francis was not perturbed about explaining their disaffection to the Baron, for it would merely further ingratiate him in the eyes of the tyrant. Of course, he did have to consider the damage Lombard might do him in an effort to prevent his own destruction.

The truculent clouds announcing the shores of the Dominion soon appeared in the last rays of the retreating sunset. Francis used the ship's lavatory to affix his formal audience mask, knowing that within a few minutes of landing he would be in the presence of the Baron. He would have liked to set it to a special setting he had commissioned from the artisan, the one he reserved for Rochalle alone, but it would not do at the busy landing site, although she would certainly be there. He wondered if any of the symptoms of childbearing would be more pronounced, the swelling of the abdomen and so forth. He had cautioned her to do as much to conceal it as possible, and to attribute the rest to a hearty appetite since the gestation of a living form by a cyborg human would certainly be entered quickly on the fatal list of Dooms, if not already so enumerated. Strange, he thought, that he had no qualms about the birth of the child. He could not really be concerned with the knowledge that it was the first such "free" birth outside the breeding kitchens and the Foundry in the last twenty centuries. He could only rejoice over the thought of *his* child. It would have been nice to have a son, but it seemed Rochalle was quite sure it was to be a girl. A girl. Coca-Cola. A name from the day before the Destruction.

The ship stirred to life around him, a great bird fluttering its wings after landing. The terminal was busy with much air traffic coming and going. It was a healthy sign, this commerce, thought Francis. The sting of winter reminded him of the cold, but so minor in intensity was the cold that he did not bundle up the heavy sark-fur parka he had brought from the Cold.

He was pleasantly surprised to see Rochalle coming toward him at the disembarkation point, but there was an intenseness about her that alerted him. Then, he saw them. At the other end of the hall he watched the guard troop marching briskly toward him. Moving forward he met Rochalle.

"They're coming for you, Francis, my darling," she said, squeezing his arm.

"I see. . . ." Quickly from under his parka he took the Cube and thrust it into her hand. "Take this and hide it . . . use your clearance. Take it to the Mirror Room."

"But Francis—"

"No time, Rochalle . . . go, before they search you."

They gazed into each other's eyes for a moment, then Francis pushed her past him into the crowd and walked toward the guards.

"Are you looking for me?" he asked calmly of the tall, black-and-orange-masked troopers.

"Sir Francis of North Dunnetowne?" said the Captain of the guard.

"Yes."

"I have my orders to place you under security control. Please follow us to our vehicle. I'm sure it is only a matter of routine, Sir Francis. After all, you have just returned from the Cold, the only returning member of a thirty-man team. Naturally, there would be questions to answer at the Citadel," explained the Captain.

"Yes," said Francis, at peace with himself knowing that the Cube was safely hidden. But he was worried about Rochalle. She probably had thought it prudent to remain sequestered from prying eyes, for he calculated she was entering her eighth month. She had taken a great chance coming out to meet him.

He recognized the security vehicle as one of the Baron's élite guard, but he did not recognize the emblems on the uniforms.

"Of what division are you, Captain?"

"Inner Citadel Corps, Sir Francis."

"Tell me, what news is there? I've been away for a time and, frankly, am bereft of any recent informations."

"I'm sorry, Sir Francis. I have been instructed to have no further communications with the prisoner."

"Prisoner?"

There came no explanation.

"Am I your prisoner?"

The vehicle entered the first perimeter and turned toward the underground. Guards activated the gate, and they entered the subterranean roadway that led to the terra incognita of the Inner Citadel. Instantly Francis knew what had happened. Lombard had engineered his arrest. It was conceivable that the Baron was ignorant of his arrival altogether.

The squad of troopers exited and formed two columns flanking either side of Francis. Marching through the metal corridors, their heavy footsteps reverberated until they reached an acoustically proofed elevator. Francis was not sure, but the motion of the elevator seemed neither to descend nor rise, the suggestion was of a horizontal rather than vertical movement. It stopped, the wall faded, and they stepped out into . . . Francis recognized it immediately. It was the Quotient of Limbo, the room Lombard used for his perverse purposes. The Spinning Room.

Noiselessly the guards left him alone in the room. The silence literally hummed around Francis. And just as soundlessly and suddenly, Lombard was there, smiling malevolently. His eyes malignant with delight, his hands fidgeting hungrily.

"Sir Francis, how good of you to drop in," Lombard leered at him.

Francis closed his eyes, praying that he could kill with his mind.

"Please, Sir Francis, I just came to say good-by."

Francis regained enough control, his mask having remained undisturbed. "Are you going somewhere?"

"Not at this moment, but I believe *you* are about to take a short and, sadly, unpleasant journey, verily unto the very shores of the River Styx itself."

Lombard's nostrils quivered. He sniffed the air exaggeratedly. "Do you smell something burning, Sir Francis?"

For a moment, Francis refused to let his mind settle on the inference Lombard had made.

"I'm sure I smell something burning. Guards, come take Sir Francis to see what's burning. Good-by, Sir Francis. I'm sure you'll appreciate the contrast. First the furies of the Cold, and now the very reverse. Fare thee well."

The guards entered and took Francis to the elevator. Before the long ride in the shaft had ended, Francis had accepted his destination and had begun formulating his course of action.

The wall fell away to reveal a different contingent of guards to whom his escort delivered Francis. He recognized well enough the insignia on their foreheads. Special Corps. Burning House Brigade. Quickly and without a single word, he was ushered to a cell, searched by the scanners, and left to himself. Francis was surprised at the cleanliness of the cell, the floor literally shone; even the cot was comfortable and a table held a container of cool water to slake his thirst.

But then it began. The nothing. No one came to question him; the lighting was slowly dimmed. There must have been something in the water, for he began to feel as if he had been there for a long time. The lights seemed to be raised and lowered, to simulate the passage of days. Artificial day after artificial day flashed by. He lost track of any time reference.

It was not long, or was it? He could not tell when he began to hear sounds, some were scratching sounds, like nails against the walls. Clanging sounds, heavy metal doors opening and closing, followed by whooshing sounds, snapping sounds, popping explosions, muffled sounds. Then the scream started.

How long the scream had been going on Francis could not tell. He soon included it in the now familiar cacophony of sounds that assailed him continuously. It must have been days. Weeks.

All the sounds were so familiar that he no longer took notice of them, but one day the scream turned into a sob, a gasp. Then the sound of the metal door clanging shut, the sputter and popping sounds. And then, nothing. The utter, absolute silence fell upon him like a lead hammer. Soon he strained his ears to the point of hearing his own electricity, the mutter of his blood through his veins. Something about the end of the scream frightened him, left him desolate.

Something burning. He sniffed. Yes, something burning. Coming from the end of the corridor. He got off his couch and went to the cell door. Still weak from the drug, his legs staggered beneath him, and he fell against the door. It swung open with his weight.

Francis tumbled onto the hard metal floor, the pain clearing his mind of some of the fog. He gathered himself up against the wall and listened. Nothing. He inched along the wall toward the end of the tubular corridor, toward the source of the sounds he had heard.

Birds beat themselves silly in the passageways of his ears, perplexed twitters and bleats issued forth. Francis pounded his hands against the door, against his ears, until the sounds came out in spurts. His body felt as if its three rhythms had hit triple critical, the transitional weakness shaking his mind apart somewhere above his neck, behind the ashen mask.

He rubbed his eyes through the ocular patches, the pressure was real and reassuring. He pushed against the metal door with his eyes, then his hands; his whole body crashed against it. He heard the door activated. It slid away.

"Did you want something?"

It was Lombard standing with a three-pronged hook. Behind him was the Burning Room, itself. Now the scream and the popping sounds grew monstrous in meaning.

"Perhaps a tour of the facility, Sir Francis. Would you come this way? You're lucky, it's cooking hour."

Too weakened to resist, Francis was easily lead into the room by two guards who wore the thickly greased aprons common to workers in the Burning House. A loud report was heard, the popping sound of earlier.

"You are curious, Sir Francis? The sound is peculiar to the quills, their heads tend to pop once they go in. But it does take them a long time to reach that point, resistant little devils they are. But the fires are hot."

Francis lurched wildly at Lombard; the guards restrained him.

"Ah, ah, Sir Francis. Please. Don't force me to lose control. It appears that you have something which I really need to have. Let us go into the observation room and discuss this matter."

Francis was strapped into the same chair into which he had seen the Captain shackled.

"Now, it has come to my attention that you have in your possession a certain device, a cube-shaped instrument given to you by the quill monster. It appears that this weapon might do some small harm to the interests of the Dominion, so we must have it from you, Sir Francis. Really we must. We've conducted a rather extensive search of your quarters and yourself, but, alas, we find it not. Perhaps you could illuminate us as to its whereabouts. Sir Francis, I'm waiting."

"Eat figs, Lombard."

"Testy, Sir Francis, very testy. Must I resort to means of exterpolation? I'm sure you're aware of our talents."

"It will do you no good, the Cube has been activated. It has been placed, well in advance of your treachery."

"You bluff poorly, Sir Francis. It could not be placed. I know the breeding ground, and it has not been affected."

"Why are you so afraid, Lombard? If you kill me, then the Cube could not be used."

"Only a half-truth, my friend. Don't be so anxious to martyr your life. We know you have many confederates who could accomplish the task."

"Sir Lombard, you're so clever to have found me out. Almost as clever as your poetry."

"Humor at a moment like this, Sir Francis? I think it is time for more sustained efforts. Guards, you may begin the interrogation. And, do hurry, leisure is not with us today."

Just as the guards were about to affix their tools, heavy steps before the door announced a visitor.

"Guard, see who it is."

"No need to see who it is," came the unmistakable booming voice.

"Baron, ah huh, a most pleasant surprise. You honor us with your presence. We were just examining our prisoner. . . ."

"Is that not Sir Francis behind that prisoner's mask?"

"Why, yes, Baron, it is."

"Why was I not informed of his arrival?"

"We thought it prudent to interrogate him as soon as possible inasmuch as he has been in such recent and intimate contact with our enemies."

The massive form of the Baron approached the couch where Francis feebly turned his head, too weak to speak.

"So, Sir Francis, you seem to be in a most unenviable position. Our zealous Lombard would have you represented as an enemy of the state. Unstrap him guards."

"But, Baron, he's very dangerous."

"My orders."

The guards hurried to untie the limp arms of Francis.

"Some of my guard will deliver him to his own chambers to wait my pleasure."

"Baron, may I caution you most earnestly about the serpentine glibness of this man's tongue. He'll seek to incite you against many of your most loyal subjects with bizarre tales. Don't be persuaded by his evil delirium of words."

"Lombard, you protest too fervently. I will speak to you later. Now go!"

"But, Baron—"

"No more, Lombard. I warn you."

"Yes, Baron, as you please."

"Guards, carry Sir Francis to his rooms. See to it that he is cared for properly. And . . . send for his consort."

Q

His chambers had never seemed more comfortable. The walls glowed with warm green, a healing color selected by the physician. Already the stale imprint of the Burning House cell was fading. Climbing the spirals of his mind toward recovery, Francis felt the entrance of Rochalle before she spoke.

"Rochalle," he said, without opening his eyeholes.

"Yes, Francis, I am here."

Francis looked in the direction of her voice. Someone new was standing there. A woman with a strange disproportion and an even stranger radiance emanating from her in all directions.

Rochalle approached Francis on his couch and touched his forehead with her hand.

"Rochalle," said Francis, "it grows within you."

"Yes. Put your hand here, you can feel the movement."

"I can feel it. So much movement; it must be soon."

"Within one week, I think."

"You look well, Rochalle. It suits you, this childbearing."

"I have missed you, Francis. Rest now."

"I cannot rest. Did you not see the guards outside the door? I am under close arrest."

"I saw no guards. The Baron himself sent the physician. His mask was most pleasant."

"Then perhaps the Baron is aware of the menace. Perhaps Lombard has not been able to convince him."

"What is all this about, Francis?"

"There is too much to tell, and I think the less you know the safer you will be. What of the Cube?"

"What is the significance of the Cube? I hid it as you asked, but what does it mean? The physician said you kept mentioning it in your fitful sleep."

"Only the Baron must know. Help me ready myself for an audience with him. Here, help me, Rochalle."

"I cannot. Medication has been administered. You suffer from exhaustion. You must rest."

"The Baron must know."

"Yes, Francis. Tomorrow. It can wait till the morrow. Rest. Rest, my dear Francis."

It was closer to three days before Francis gained full consciousness, but he was thankful. All his strength and energy had been reinstated. He was up and prepared to meet the Baron just as the squad of guards activated the portal.

"Sir Francis, the Baron will see you."

"Yes, I am coming. Excellent timing."

"Sir?"

"Never mind. Let us go."

Q

The Baron stood in the high archway of the leaded-glass window, surveying the courtyard below, heavy metal gauntlets clasped behind his back.

"Sir Francis of North Dunnetowne," announced the attendant.

Without turning after the announcement, the Baron motioned Francis to his side.

"Sir Francis, look below. What do you see?"

"I see . . . gunships, hundreds of gunships."

"Yes. An armada to blacken the skies."

"Where do they go?"

"To meet the brunt of the quill invaders. They are on the march. By land, by sea, but we have air superiority. They will not see the shores of the Dominion. Perhaps their blood will lap against the gray rocks with the tide."

"There is a far greater menace than the quill invaders."

"You must mean the Spore."

"But, yes . . ."

"Look at those troopers. Brave men all."

"They needn't die."

"The cream of the Dominion. Every last division committed to this final action. Only the Burning House goons kept in reserve."

"Is that wise?"

"It was necessary. Intelligence reported that conditions warranted full commitment."

"Lombard did this."

"Watch them lift from the ground, Sir Francis. Birds that must never touch earth lest they die. Wave upon wave of doomed men."

"You fear that we will lose, that the invaders will vanquish us?"

"Is there any doubt in your mind, Sir Francis?"

"But, Baron, I don't understand."

"There will be no winners, Sir Francis. Neither our forces nor those of the Quill. Look, the very skies bulge with our brood."

The mirrorlike armor of the Baron flowed with the passing air fleets.

"Behold, Sir Francis, the end of an Age."

"But if neither army finalizes a victory, who then?"

"The Spore."

"But that need not be. I have a weapon to destroy them. I need only locate their breeding point."

"Is this true, Sir Francis?"

"Yes, and there is still time."

"Where is this weapon?"

"I have it safely away, but I will fetch it."

"Do so now. I will recall my forces if you can convince me of this weapon against the Spore."

Francis dashed across the grounds to his chamber and gathered the necessary articles he would need for securing the Cube. Rochalle was there, heavy with child.

"Where are you going, Francis?"

"To retrieve the Cube. I can forestall the war if it succeeds, and I trust the word of the Quill."

"What is this Cube?"

"I told you before. It would be dangerous for you to know."

"Can I not go with you?"

"Be reasonable, Rochalle. Your condition . . . the child."

"You are right, Francis. I will remain here for your return. Please be careful."

"I will."

After Francis had left, Rochalle lifted her womb onto the couch, eyes staring overhead, thinking of the Cube as she held the movement between her hands.

"You can come out now. He's gone," she said.

A slow shuffling weight followed by the sound of wet, sliding limbs supporting a great mass crept out of the rear compartment.

"You need not fear the Cube," said the strange voice attached.

"I do not fear the Cube. It is not a weapon, but a tool of discovery."

"It grows well?" asked the voice towering above Rochalle.

"Yes, it grows well," answered Rochalle, feeling her swollen abdomen, a small warm smile on her vermilion lips. "The Spore grows well. . . ."

Q

Cloaked by the night, Francis felt his way along the passage-way. As he descended into the winding corridors of the Inner Citadel, the sense of claustrophobia bore heavily upon him.

Veins gorged and disgorged with blood, heated with adrenalin. Moisture clung along the brow brims of his mask and seeped into his eyeholes, blinding him at times. Swiftly his heart shrank and swelled beneath his tunic as he neared the Hall of the Mirror.

The fourteen sets of guards were easily passed upon showing the Baron's personal insignia. Guaranteeing his mobility, the pass also lent him access to the dungeons, the armory, the room of pain, and the Mirror itself. Once in a dream he had told himself to go seek out this mirror and face his flesh face. With his reflector grille set in place before his mask, Francis drew the door away and entered the Mirror.

Where everyone else would have perished, Francis survived the Mirror's power by his reflector. Mirror saw Mirror ad infinitum and he was able to pass undestroyed. Countless beams of refracted and defracted light bombarded his eyeholes, in vain. Guardians of the true Mirror, the beams crisscrossed the path to the source of all light. He entered the Infinite Regression with immunity.

It was here that Francis had Rochalle hide the Cube where others could not go, for it was a mirror to be faced only by the one who wore a face of flesh, thus had the ancient bequeathers of the Mirror wrought.

Every fiber of his body vibrated with the energy thrusting at him from all sectors as he reached the apex of the Mirror. At the very focal point of its rays, Francis reached for the Cube. His hands felt along the almost tangible beams, they reached out for the source of deliverance, the hope, the . . . his hands grasped emptiness. The Cube was gone.

Q

Atop the foam-rippled swell, the Great Quill floated, a leviathan of unperturbable visage, drifting with the tide that would take him into the main current. All about, he sensed and communicated with the thousands of his followers, the sea quill, all who trumpeted their support. Like great bags of sea vegetation, the inundating waves of sea quill covered the waters. At night their bodies glowed softly, some blue, some green, others orange and red, according to their age and maturity.

The Great Quill was aware of the land, the small rocks dotting the surface of the world. Upon these specks of solidity, armies of land quill and their man allies strove across the geographical barriers of forest and mountain. A single great song lifted from the ocean lanes, a harmony of strange voices, as if some huge creature breathed and exhaled, humming some mild tune to while away the time.

The Great Quill now had reached his full growth and easily dwarfed any of his fellow creatures, yet he was borne along by the waters as if he were the lightest of feathers. Still, those sea quill who tired could swim to him and attach themselves to him so that they might be buoyed up by his great size and strength. Often many were joined to him this way, each time leaving refreshed and joyous from the intimacy of their contact with the Great Quill.

As the ocean swelled up around them, brain bags floated out from the land, curious at the change of color; so had the quill mottled the water's surface. Airy lanterns, the brain bags rose and fell, riding the currents of air, forming a canopy over the silently marching army, floating its way to war.

Far away over the horizon, the Great Quill could already hear the drone of the gunships, still hours away. He sighed and sank a little lower in the lapping wavelets. The vision of the carnage to come saddened him. The obliteration of the nest, the destruction of his people and that of the enemy, all of it as irrevocable as the tides.

As the night came heavily, obscuring one from the other, the multitudes called out to one another, their innumerable limbs bemoaning the strangeness of the night. They hurried toward the center of their midst, toward the hub and the Great Quill himself. Like the arms of an immense pinwheel, they clung to each other, the current spinning the great wheel of their corporate bodies toward the outcropping of rock ahead. Aglow with their luminescence, the living spiral floated against the backdrop of stars and galaxies overhead.

Q

The Spore vessel hung motionless above the planet. The starship shuddered as in sympathetic labor pains for the cycle being fulfilled far below. Convulsions, two thousand years dormant, shook through the undulating, amorphous form in delicate response to the heavings of life below. As in all things, the recycling was about to begin. The tenure of permanence had run to the end of its lease on the world, and now the dip of the curve below the line of transition would once more tip the poles from up to down. Complete in the essay of birth and death, the cycle lay within the folds of sheer energy.

The Spore ship roused itself, speaking to its members as if waking from long and restful slumber. Round about the ship, liquid globules of coagulated honeyed dust now were culled and curried for sons and daughters forming up in queues and columns. Heedless of the warnings of oracles and sages, the tapestry of life on the planet below had long sneered its defiance at the bulge of space, the great emptiness engulfing them in a cosmic ocean. A flood tide had crested the walls of sanity, running out first as small rivulets and streams, soon to be a torrent rushing over the face of the world, the entire solar system itself.

Q

Francis bore the emptiness of his hands well. Well enough that Rochalle seemed not to apprehend the grave despair within his mind. He entered the chamber and drew a cushion to sit by her.

"Did all go well, Francis? Is the Cube safe?"

Francis just shook his head and laid it disconsolately upon the bedside near Rochalle's long fingers.

"It was gone, someone had taken it." He could not see her face, which was gripped by much torment.

"I promised the Baron that the Cube would save us from the Spore, from the war greeting itself out over the ocean, but I've failed and the world dies with me. I cannot stop it now."

"Perhaps it is for the better," she said quietly.

"What can you mean?"

"A cleansing, Francis. A newness transformed from the carnal house of anger and violence. Let the world die, Francis. From its rich humus, a new world will sprout."

"Our people, the quill . . . just to let the blotting out happen, I cannot stand idly by while the world implodes upon itself."

"But, Francis, you struggle for consciousness. Let the world fall asleep. Death is not painful, only the process. Don't prolong the dying. The world has died before and yet it lives."

"But the child . . . how can you so eagerly sacrifice our child?"

"The child?"

"Yes, the child growing within you now."

"But what can you do, Francis? The Cube is lost."

"Perhaps I can still find the Spore breeding ground. It must be housed within the Citadel, else Lombard would not remain here to supervise the incubation."

"Do you think it possible, Francis?"

"I must try."

"And if you find the breeding ground, will you destroy it?"

"Utterly. With its destruction the world need not be inherited by the meek. The answer lies not in the Baron, nor in the Innisfree dream, nor in the Great Quill, himself. And strangely enough, I think the Quill knew this, too. I would have liked you to meet him. He wasn't so bad if you could accustom yourself to his face."

"Why do you struggle so, Francis? Why not let Fate have its way?"

"I've always struggled. I've killed. I don't feel remorse, regret. Those I killed would kill. Death . . . so what? Some thought it a better profession than the other professional diers; those who waited for a cancer to go malignant, or snatched up by some other vagary of Fate. I don't care about all this smoothly running order and harmony. Are we game pieces, toy conundrums, playthings in the hands or minds of others, whispering their wills through our mouths? Some men see galaxies in pine knots, others broil death in a spoon. Not I. Although I may not know where infinity begins or ends, or its warp and woof, although I cannot count unborn chromosomes or lead you to the place where quills drag themselves to die, I will tell you this. I will work death in my hands before I give up my life."

"Then your choice is made. Go, Francis, do what you can."

"I have made my choice and I am going. And I just may die."

"Francis, your child will live. It will carry you into the future. You will not die. Never for me will you die."

"Rochalle, do not become angry with me. I thank you for those kind . . . pleasantries. Yes, for pleasantries are what they were, to me. The child may live, he may not. If I die, I will never know. If I live, yes, there will be a child, a new life, but none to which I lay claim of any kind. Its life will be of a sovereignty, as any other's. This notion of kin, of relationship, never became part, or rather, it never convinced me of its authenticity. Bonds are by choice, not by chances of birth. Mother, father, child . . . these are words, only words to me. They carry no magic connotation, no divine oracular message. It simply doesn't affect me. So, please, let us not construe any substitutional myth. I would feel better about it."

"As you wish, Francis."

"My strangling wire, do you know where it is?"
"Here."
"And my extra ammunition?"
"Pain or death?"
"Death bullets, please."

Q

As he drove, Francis felt the bullets hanging heavily in his pocket. The threat of the Spore infestation, the Armies of the Dominion and of the Quill meeting headlong, the wounds and pains harassing his body played their heavy melody. And yet there was something else, a nagging apprehension, a formless question that, nevertheless, took form in a wrinkled brow. Something . . . something was wrong, very wrong . . . somewhere.

He could not identify it, but something tugged at him, pulled at his mind's elbow.

He laid his fears aside, he concentrated on what had to be done. Either he must find the Cube weapon and with it destroy the Spore nestlings, or he would simply have to destroy it without the aid of the device. Where to begin his search?

It came again, tugging at him, distracting him. What was it? he asked himself. For a moment he thought it was a smell, but it faded before he could be sure.

He had driven out in the countryside, passing Waltham Forest, to his old bunker to which he still had access. A strong wind blew southwesterly and brought with it the chill of the marshlands as he sat on the earthen slope under which lay the small but comfortable bunker. He loaded his weapon, unslinging it from around his neck, feeding the cartridges into the butt plate. He sighted down the barrel at the seemingly sterile embankment opposite him. He fired and watched as the projectiles arched high into the air, to plummet screaming into the soil at six different places. Apparently there had been some moss or lichen, something alive, at least, to attract the death bullets.

He reloaded, assured that the weapon, unfired for so long, was fully operable. He checked the packing of the strangling wire, felt its tense coil vibrate slightly, tightly sprung into its canister on his forearm. The familiar weapons of his youth, now unfamiliar. Even his killing mask was out of fashion, old. The model was no longer in production. And for that matter, the strangling wire had been the gift of his father, but, true enough, it had served him in good stead. And the dagger, the hunting blade presented to him by the Baron so long ago. No, they weren't familiar to him, they were strange. Strange and cold in his hands. The knife in its boot sheath did not hum with that fearsome energy. It was there but like a sulking sark, obedient but not loyal. Would it kill for him as well as before? He could not know, yet his life depended on it.

He looked at his hands that carried the weapons to their tasks. Plowshares, he thought, pitted and scarred, older, older than before.

The ramshackle moon shunted its dull light across the glaze of dead water, lingering on the perimeter of the bog. The light was withered, dry as late autumn leaves in the south country. Heat lightning rolled in balls along the rotting logs, Francis' eyes following the *ignis fatuus* of his thoughts as they skipped and bounced from one possibility to another. Should he go there, or there? Should he seek out Lombard from the Burning House . . . ? He shuddered. Should he just simply wait? Wait. The word echoed in his head as it finally came to him. What was he doing in this desolate area of the city, long since abandoned to the creeping muck tides?

A feeling inundated him, covering him with the sense of utter stillness, as if nothing moved; no wind . . . no sound . . . every object stood bereft of time's passage. The dimension of time was gone. He took hold of himself, reminding himself of the trickster within everyone, the game player that shared the company of actors within his consciousness. It wanted him to be afraid, to fear the inanimate night, the illusion that he was out of time, *somewhere else.*

He reminded himself of fabrications of the mind, confused perceptions and the deprivations of sleep, inadequate food. It was beginning to tell on him physically and mentally. He tried to concentrate on Rochalle's image; it helped. The hum came back to life, he could feel and hear and sense the bubbling of the ethers, the churning of matter and energy all about him. The feeling had passed.

He had no time to consider the ramifications of the experience. The dagger began to jerk within his boot, whispering, muttering as it was wont when an enemy was in range of its sensors. The Quotient of Limbo. The thought leapt into his mind just as the dagger flew to his hand, quaking, the killing being near. The experience had been much like the interrogation machine. The knife began to scream, "Kill! Kill! Kill!" and strike out at the vacant air violently. It was all Francis could do to restrain the mad slashing at the invisible enemy. Wrestling his knife arm to his side and with a great wrench of will, Francis made his hand spring open, dropping the knife to the earth where it flopped and screamed in a frenzy like a dying fish.

Obviously the knife had gone mad with disuse. Francis walked away from it, far enough away until he could no longer hear the gasping cries. Soon it was very quiet. Francis walked deeper in the moonlit forest, listening to the soft crunch of twigs and needles beneath his boots and feeling more at ease than he had for quite some time. His path took him up the gentle slope of a low, rounded hill, perhaps a small salt dome, for he could hear the muffled echoes of his footfalls within the chambered mound.

The curtain of scraggly trees, dwarf pines, fell away toward the very crest of the hill, revealing the panorama of London sprawling below. The bowl of the valley emptied down into the murky distance, past the fetid trickle of the Thames. Ever so often a brain bag would lift off from a tree and cause a flash of light in the darkness as it floated over the darker portions of the city's suburbs. A lone gunship patrolled the farthest corner of the perimeter, its flashprobe poking a smokey hole through the darkness. Here and there a campfire betrayed a colony of vagrants in the condemned sections of the city. All in all, it was an interesting view from his newfound vantage point.

All the problems were down there, congested within the environs of vestigial history, a museum of the past, buried in its own decay. Yet, Francis knew that he loved it, loved the gritty buildings, the clogged streets, the raucous taverns. He could remember his first sight of the city when his father had brought him into the service of the Baron as apprentice assassin so many years ago. In those less turbulent days the streets had been thronged with travelers, pilgrims, troupes of musicians, caravans of pack quill, tradesmen hawking their wares above the din of noise and commotion.

Now the city lay dark and unmoving beneath the blackout ordered by the Baron. The gunship began enforcing the order by snuffing out the errant brain bags; soon even the campfires disappeared. Lying back on the tufts of tough grass, Francis folded arm under arm and closed his eyes, joining the darkness with darkness. He closed his eyes but still he could see the city, the gray smudge of rusting metal and pitted stone, far more beautiful in his mind than the glistening bell-shaped cities being grown out in the wild heather land to the north and the east. Even now he knew that much of the population had moved into the areas surrounding the new cities, vacating the great city below, leaving it to the wandering scavengers and sark packs. He imagined they would soon leave the city itself, probably break into the line of bunkers vacated by the troops now winging their way to their fate. Then, after the vagrants had moved on when the food ran out, the quill would return, reoccupy their old lands, fulfilling the old prophecy. Francis smiled to himself at the irony of it all.

With or without the war, the quill would win. Francis shook his head at the senseless battle brewing out over the ocean. Could not the fools see their true enemy, the Spore, the subjugation of both their races by the ubiquitous Spore, the threat eating into the very fabric of their lives? It seemed as if the Baron and the Great Quill wished their peoples to suffer the slow death which would follow the destruction of the sea by the Spore legions on the verge of hatching somewhere. Somewhere. Where? Perhaps it was underground or in an orbital chamber. Below his feet or above him. Or maybe somewhere in-between or under the ocean. The possibilities were infinite. How could he ever find the breeding place in time? St. Agnes's Eve; when was it? Two days and a few tattered hours hence.

From his isolated position on the hill and all the usual signs of life below, Francis could easily imagine himself the last man on earth, plodding from city to town, from town to village, in the never-ending search for water, the once great watery world a parched desert.

Far from fantasy he turned his eyes from the listless clouds overhead. Rochalle would like it here, he thought. It would be a pleasant place to erect a small living chamber; the child would benefit from the space and solitude although it was a bit bleak. But they could move the tree, have it replanted and perhaps later locate some of those flower seeds and soil to nurture them. It would cost a great deal, but he could think of nothing more important.

Yes, a small living bell here, and they could incorporate the hollow chamber beneath for a bunker in case of pillaging bands of vagrants. It would be nice to have one of those young quill females to care for the child. He could remember his childhood fond memories, although his general revulsion for the quills made him sigh for the tolerance of his childhood.

Yes, Rochalle and the child would like it here. It wasn't entirely out of the question; after all, they might survive.

Again his trained mind became perplexed and forced the question upon itself. What am I doing here? "The world is dying," he said out loud. "What am I doing here?"

"The world? the world? Why there are so many, many more; come, we'll plunder in tether through cosmic gore."

The voice seemed to emanate from the very rock upon which Francis rested. The ringing echo flung itself back and forth, bringing Francis to his feet, weapon scanning the area. When he saw no one he fired a burst, trusting the death bullets to seek out their target. They arched overhead, hung searching, then fell screaming into the upturned belly of the hill.

The entire hill quaked as one enormous stomach, rolling with laughter. The ground began to vibrate, shake, then heave itself in a great lumbering movement. Suddenly Francis realized that the hill itself was some immense camouflaged creature, now just beginning to rouse itself. Francis fell away, rolling to the gully below. The wind knocked from him, dust in his eyes, Francis could easily ascribe the vision he saw to incipient madness.

Stone and dirt falling from its monstrous bulk, the incredible behemoth shook itself clean of the debris, Francis being part of it. It stretched its great clawed forepaws, shook out its wings, rubbing its stomach where the bullets had struck.

Francis recovered himself enough to reaim his weapon and was about to fire again when the leviathan called out, "Please, don't do that again; there really is no need."

With weapon still at the ready, Francis sighted down the barrel and asked, "What are you? What do you want?"

"Very basic questions as to identity and purpose, very linear logic. Well, what do you think I am? Come on, guess."

Francis began to squeeze the trigger.

"Now, now, don't lose your sense of humor. But, of course, you're intimidated by the size difference. You are concerned that I may step on you or sneeze in your direction. Fear not."

"What do you want with me? You must be the reason I'm here; I can't think of any other."

"Right you are there; I did call for you."

"Well, what is it? Get on with it; my short patience is in even shorter supply."

"Can't you guess, Sir Francis? It's fairly obvious."

"Well, portions of your appearance hint at quillish blood, others seem quasi-human, still others—parts are utterly alien to me. Alien? Are you Spore?"

"The what? Spore?"

"Is this the hatchery, the breeding ground for the Spore aliens? And you are one of them!" His trigger finger trembled with emotion.

"Perhaps we should discuss 'manifestations,' Sir Francis. I think the concept is germaine to the topic at hand. Yes, manifestations. In my present form, there are obviously elements disturbing to your usual, ordinary frames of reference; number one being the factor of dimension. I think we can eliminate that factor, remove one stumbling block and so forth; after all, size is only relative, it being in the eye of the beholder. Let me see, yes, there. How is that, now? Much better, our seeing eye to eye, that is."

Through some unexplained means Francis found himself facing the creature in miniature, literally eye to eye. It was not a great deal more comforting for he could now easily discern various and sundry surface anomalies which made the creature even more disconcerting if not threatening in aspect.

"Hi, ho, that is better. Let me readjust a moment, the altitude, you know, stifles the sinuous membranes. Excuse me."

Little arms and legs, wings, tentacle, teeth, heads seemed to appear and disappear in profusion on the skin of the creature, reminding Francis of Innisfree and the pleasure domes and their constantly melding images. The thing was more horrible in its human size, a chimera of bizarre parts and glistening tusks upcurled.

"No, I'm not this Spore you speak of, not in the technical sense, at least . . . but I could be if you put enough into it. Right now your emanations are confused; you don't have in mind any particular focused image. Now if you could get the image together, I'll be able to better manifest it for you."

"Where have you come from?"

"From? Hmmm, yes, well spatial considerations all in all, I suppose it would suffice to say I've always been here, more or less where you found me, disguised as this hill."

"You mean, your capacity has been that of a hill? But what is your avowed purpose, your goal in life?"

"A hill today, but I, also, was a boy, a bush, and a scaly fish in the sea. Now, I might become you or you could become me."

"I don't fathom any of this. Why did you call for me?"

"Call for you . . . ? Yes, called for you. Well, it amounts to this, somewhat more than a molehill . . . haha . . . ha? Not funny, eh? Well, I can see you are taking this all very seriously and I'm being frivolous and rude. I am your greatest hopes, your greatest fears, the ghost of St. Agnes's Eve Future, the demon from the Mirror living therein, the fire, the ritual, the offering; the seed and the sown as well as the harvest."

"Riddles, parables. Tell why you brought me here to this macabre rendezvous or, by the Great Flood, I'll empty my weapon into you. I think the bullets big enough now to do more than tickle your ribs."

"But, Sir Francis, where is your historical perspective, your sanity-saving humor, the good will you proffered toward your peoples? You would do me harm merely because my words run together? Hear me out, please."

"Speak."

"Shall we return to the original question? Why have I arranged for our meeting? Let me tell you a story by way of preface, Sir

Francis. Once upon a time, somewhat before the First Time, about five thousand years ago, what you call the Legendary Period, somewhere beyond the rim of this whirlpooling galaxy, a large space ship was traversing deep space. It had just returned from a highly successful engagement to a neighboring galactic confederation of solar systems. The nature of its enterprise, and that of the beings on board, was business and adventure.

"It had been on a safari to some very far-flung planetary systems to gather specimens both for scientific research and for exhibition purposes on their long trek to their home planet. . . . Sir Francis, maybe it would help if you would concentrate on a close individual so that I might assume his shape to better facilitate our communication? Perhaps a girl. Have you one in mind?"

"I prefer to see you as you are, creature. Continue your story although I do not apprehend its relevancy."

"As I am? But that's rather difficult, for you see I am not in a state of is-ness, being, you know. I only exist as long as you believe in me. And please don't call me creature, for although it may well apply, I prefer a more familiar appellation. Please call me Froth."

"All right, Froth, so be it. The story."

"Yes, the story. Well, the starship with its crew and cargo of rare and strange beings from many different planets had completed its last engagement and had chartered a course for home. Fated, it took a short cut through this solar system. A monumental explosion ripped the sun's surface, sending a jet of solar flame gushing out. Caught in that fatal flood, the very flood you honor by your epithet, the starship was torn asunder. Its crew and multitudinous specimens were hurtled out of the protective envelope of the starship into the deadly vacuum of space. The void engulfed their life energies and spread them out with the rays of light scattered eons ago by long-extinct stellar furnaces."

"They died, is what you're saying."

"Yes, they . . . died. However, among these various and sundry creatures a particularly tenacious creature, actually, two of these, a couple of the others, and a single crewman somehow managed to survive in a sealed section of the ravaged craft. Now a piece of space debris, it drifted into the magnetic tides that brought it to a planet, into an orbit which eventually decayed, allowing for the wreckage to reach the surface where the survivors, in varying stages of physical and mental health, escaped once they learned that the atmosphere and such was supportive of their biosystems. They took various paths all of which over the centuries spread wider in their divergence. And the outcome of all this is—"

"That you are one of the surviving creatures escaped from this zoo ship."

"Not quite, Sir Francis. You see, I am the lucky crew member who escaped. Yes, sigh, escaped. For you see, Sir Francis, *you* are one of the zoo specimens or rather their descendant. Little beasties who escaped from their cages, more or less. And the quill, too."

"At this point . . . Froth, I could care less about my five-millennia-old parentage; it would seem to make very little difference. Is it safe to assume that you have been lying around dormant all this time?"

"Oh, but no, I've been very active, that is, in the legendary period and occasionally during the First Time, but this is my inaugural visit into the Second Time. I've been this hill for the last two thousand years. Actually, I used to be quite an imposing mountain, all snow peaked and such, but I weathered, lost a good deal of mass while I hibernated. Are you beginning to piece together anything from all this, Sir Francis?"

"Something about the two-thousand-year cycle; I can relate that to the timetable set up by the Spore and for the proscribed reign of the Baron. There seems to be a mergence of trends here. You, the Spore, the Baron—"

"And yourself, don't forget to include yourself in the great pattern unfolding."

"How so?"

"Now to the very gist of it all. Let's talk about a tangential but relevant subject—life spans. Now, let's say at the present rate of exchange you can count on fifty years, we'll discount the quill, and give them about forty since they've been subjugated. Of course the Great Quill himself is another exception to the rule. That leaves me, Froth, the Meek. I simply plan to inherit the earth. I don't even have a life span. Simply put, I occupy only the present moment and have no dealings with the past or the future time dimensions, the rest of you being subject to its ravages."

"You're saying that you will just remain about until we all kill ourselves off, but haven't you forgotten the Spore? You'll have to contend with them. I believe there is a conflict of interests there, they having similar designs on the planet. And there is but one of you."

"Ah, yes, the Spore, the little devils, but I'm not unfamiliar with them. After all, we did a good deal of traveling in the old days, hopping from solar colony to binary system, planet after planet. The Spore enjoyed our show as much as the rest. We often visited their home world, a dreary place to say the least. So you're in error there.

"Also, concerning my number. As you recall I can be many things, from eggplant to mountain. You can see the City below, encircled by that chain of hills. Very pretty. Can you guess what lies just beneath the soil of those numerous hills?"

"More of your kind? The whole City surrounded by great crushing aliens waiting for the signal to advance and destroy the City."

"No, just some hills. I am the only one. But I think one of me is enough."

"I'm beginning to think so, too. Maybe even one of you is too much. Well, why did you want to make contact with me?"

"I decided to break silence, come above ground so to speak, so to speak, yes, that's it. Every two thousand years or so, we of my kind must lift up our voices, vocalize so as to reaffirm our existence by the intonation of the primeval words. It's a vibration, a harmonious utterance that massages the ethers, much as labor contractions within the female massage the newborn into life. We, I, need the reciprocal vibration, that cosmic echo to keep my being in the delicate balance it occupies twixt the dimensions."

"But what do you want with me, I repeat?"

"Are you not in the process of saving your world from disaster or making such an attempt? Are you not an individual of extraordinary tenacity and motivation? Is this not a grand stage for the reaffirmation of the basic laws of the universe, the basic laws to which all men, all quill, even all Spore must adhere? Let me ask you one more question; we have spoken of the meek inheriting the earth . . ."

"I always thought that referred to cockroaches."

"Not so, Sir Francis, and I take the inference with good humor. The meek. Is not the Great Quill, the Harbinger, meek? Surely he is, no one can deny that? But what would the Great Quill want with the world, really; he is above all those considerations. And who does that leave, the number-two meekest creature on the face of the planet?"

"Froth, the Meeker."

"Yes, Froth the Dispassionate. Froth the Crux, the architect and archetype. It was I who set the chain of cause and effect into motion, the equal cause for every equal cause. The armies soon to clash, the Baron, the nightmare Spore. Who are they but actors upon the stage? And you, Sir Francis, the leading star. Soon it will be time for bouquets and applause. Sadly enough, it is a one-act play given only one performance before the stage lights go off for the last time. There is nothing you can do about it, Sir Francis. But . . . since I am of a wagering nature, since I've always been a gambler and found my wisdom in the insecurity of it all, I have called you here to cast lots for the world. More accurately, a game of chance. Are you interested?"

"I'm interested."

"Good, well, then . . . Here are the rules: If you can locate and depose the Spore hatching grounds within one rotational cycle of this planet, I relinquish all claims to it and resume my formal role as country slope. If you fail, well, then the conclusion is obvious. I win. You all lose."

"But, what chance have I? I am no better off in my search than before coming upon you."

"But, Sir Francis, you interrupted me before I could finish. I wish to bestow upon you a certain gift, a magic wand, so to speak, to aid you in your quest for the unholy Spore. A little box. Here, take it."

"The Cube. You—"

"Please, no displays of gratitude. . . ."

"You stole it from me."

"No, I merely recovered it, intercepted it in flight, actually. One of your friends had it."

"A man named Lombard, eh? I should have known."

"No, Lombard wasn't the name; it was a female, the name being . . . Rochalle. Yes, Rochalle."

"You lie. Rochalle is my consort. I only recently left her side, she is heavy with child. The child is to be born soon."

"Sir Francis, I would suggest you hurry on; you haven't much time to find the Spore hatchery."

"You fiend, you're not implying that Rochalle is—"

"I'm not implying anything; I'm only suggesting you make haste. Remember, time is short, the world could be dead before you get back."

Q

Francis had taken the Cube and returned to his vehicle by the bunker entrance. He sat in the command chair for a moment, took in a deep breath, and pressed the ignition. Roaring through the charred countryside Francis made straightaway for his chambers in the Citadel. The growing horror in his mind made his leaden foot press heavily upon the accelerator. So many of his fears began to coalesce, the nagging questions in the back of his mind promoting the examination of the possibility that somehow Rochalle was involved in the conspiracy. Had she not attempted to dissuade him from seeking out the Spore; had she not cajoled him into letting the world fall its own way without "interfering"?

Images flashed through his mind in rapid succession; the rise of the hill which had unmasked the giant alien, the swollen abdomen of Rochalle, the teeming insect nest squirming with plump larval creatures. He shuddered, felt almost ill, as he failed

to suppress the image of Rochalle's innards housing the ravenous
Spore hatchlings making ready for exit from her body.

He remembered her questions about the Cube and how odd it
was that she could bear young internally. Yet he had accepted
it all, blindly. Just as he had passed over the disclosure that the
original Rochalle had been murdered and this new Rochalle was
a placebo, a spy, a rank imitation in the employ of the ghoulish
Lombard. But he had been persuaded by her words of love, her
smiling face, and warm embraces. How easily he had forgotten
and forgiven her; it amazed him now. Perhaps he had been
drugged, narcotized into malleability for the purposes of the
Spore. His anger and feeling of betrayal hardened into cold
resolve. He checked the chambers of his weapon for death bullets.

What had the Froth called it? The world is a stage. And what
had he been? Not the actor, the dupe. Yes, the dupe.

Q

When he entered his living chambers in the Citadel complex
he found not Rochalle, but the Baron, who stood arrayed in full-
battle armor, his silver-inlaid weapon slung round his massive
shoulders.

"Sir Francis, it is good to see you at this rather late date. I had
expected that you would be more prepared to lead the final encounter with the quill than you seem. You do not seem fully
equipped, yet I can see you do have your killing mask on. Still
we must hurry, my gunship hovers above the courtyard; the
others wait massed and ready at the farthest edge of the Dominion. The Quill and his legions are in sight, have already swept
across Innisfree to our northern perimeter, meeting no resist-
ance whatsoever from those Free Islander quislings at Glasgow.
The dogs merely stepped aside and let that army of revised lepers
and malignant dwarfs march through their land. The strategy
I've employed is to cut through the floating armada of quill to
the very vortex of that repugnant mass and slice the Great Quill
himself to ribbons, just like so many slivers of meat, to be carried
on our lances. At the sight of this, the land armies will quail and

lose heart, scatter like the dogs they are, back into the bogs and caves which spawned them.

"Come, Sir Francis, the hour draws nigh. Arm yourself with your best weapons, the children of the Dominion wait for us."

"But, Baron, the Spore. I am close to the source of the enemy. Soon I will be able to destroy the menace."

"Sir Francis, the enemy is out there, by the tens of thousands. There is no time to waste."

"But the enemy is within. Here, perhaps in the very Citadel itself. By far the Spore is the greater menace. What will we have but a hollow victory if we were to vanquish the quill only to return to the jaws of a slow Spore death? Give me time to cover our rear, you guard the flanks. Lead the armies out, but let me stay behind to follow up the final victory. I beg you for the sake of the whole land."

"Very well, Sir Francis, although I am not fully convinced of the seriousness of the matter. The Spore never made any mention of such a reprisal. We have our agreement, sealed twenty centuries ago. But, perhaps, it is well to have you remain to protect the home grounds in my absence. It is agreed."

"May you be rich with quill pelts when you return, Baron."

"And good hunting to you, Sir Francis. Do not let your elusive prey deceive you."

As Francis watched from a window overhead, the Baron's gleaming hulk strode out through the arch of triumph below in the courtyard. The gunship dipped slightly as his great mass came aboard. Soon the Baron's command ship was only a flashing red light and a faint siren's wail as it flew out over the City. Francis watched it until he could no longer discern its presence in the brown clouds. Even after the years of close association with the Baron, he still did not feel comfortable in his presence even though the ferocity of his masks had evolved to ones of less frightening visage.

Silver-toned messenger peals summoned him from a wall phone. Teeter-tottering on the balls of his feet, Francis felt as if something was compelling him to ignore the call. With a *tsk* he rejected the intuitive impulse and activated the phone.

"Hello. Yes, Sir Francis here. Rochalle, is that you? Where are you?" Francis' voice went grim. "Stay there; I'll be there in a moment. Stay there."

Q

He didn't really want to know, he admitted. Would he find the remnants of Rochalle, the feasting ground for the abominations that would thirst the world to death? Could she truly be in that unholy alliance with the Spore Aliens? He gripped his hand weapon and opened the door to the chambers, where she waited.

"Francis, are you safe?"

"Yes."

"Why do you stare so?"

"Are you in the pains?"

"Yes, they have started, every few moments now. Here, put your hand here, you can feel the kicking."

Francis refused his hand.

Suddenly Francis smelled one and turned, raising his weapon to the forebrain of the large quill that came from the blind side of his sight.

"Don't, Francis. She is my midwife, to help in the delivery of the child."

Francis slowly brought the sights of his gun down from its centered target.

"Can you trust these quill in such a matter? Better lock the weapons cabinet."

"Francis!?"

"I am not satisfied with the situation. Send her away. I wish to speak to you privately."

Rochalle sang. The quill left the room with a slow heave.

Francis did not move, spoke blankly.

"You know the quill language, Rochalle? You can communicate in their own language? When did you learn this?"

"She has been teaching me a few words, if you call them words. It's really amazingly simple. Somehow she used my own voice to teach me—I can't explain it."

Francis remembered his sojourn at the underground installation, the old quill magician, and what ensued. He knew what she could not explain.

"Why did you not tell me of the quill being employed?"

"She has been here some time, but since you were so much concerned about the problems of state, I've kept her discreetly out of view."

"I see. What else have you concealed from my awareness, Rochalle?"

"I don't understand what you mean, Francis. I have concealed nothing."

"The fig you haven't!"

Francis paced the room in extreme agitation.

"What *is* the matter, Francis?"

Francis stopped his pacing, turned his mask of wrath up to full intensity. "What is growing there, Rochalle? What horror do you nurture there in your traitorous womb?"

"Francis, what are these cruel words? What have I done to so offend you, my lord? Please, tell me."

"Do you not breed the Spore larva within you? Are you not the depository for the vile creatures, spawn-things?"

Rochalle shook her head in disbelief, her hands covering her sobbing face. "Why do you persecute me with such accusations? What have I done?"

"What have you done indeed, Rochalle? I shall have to find out the truth."

A horrible glow filled Francis' old killing mask. His hand clutched the crimson dagger. "I will cut the horror from your body!"

He raised the knife above her head as she fell back onto the sleeping couch. He plunged the knife.

His arm was caught in mid-air, the dagger falling to the floor. Francis was lifted into the air, dangling by his arm, slowly turning around until he came face to face with the quill.

"Don't hurt him," he heard Rochalle call. "Please, put him down."

The quill released Francis and picked up the dagger jerking

spasmodically on the floor, put it into its mouth, and swallowed. The knife screamed once before it disappeared into the tusk-lined cavern.

Francis felt drained, exhausted; he slumped into a chair and stared blankly ahead. The quill stood beside him, watching. Rochalle stood up and came over to him, cradling his head in her arms. She began to sing to him, softly, soothingly.

"I would have killed you," said Francis.

"I understand, Francis. It was too much to bear. You thought . . . I can understand. But it is your child I carry, nothing else. Soon you will see him. Within the day you will see the child, the father of the man."

"I am sorry, Rochalle, truly sorry. I do not know what madness overtook me. I put on my old mask and—"

"Then remove, cast it aside. I will help you."

"But I have no other mask with me. Shall I wear my face of flesh?"

"Yes, it is time that you do, Francis. Here, let me help you. Francis, your face of flesh is your weapon. The Cube. Remember, face to the Third, Face *Cubed*. Do it. Be free! Take it off!"

"I don't know if I can do it."

"The quill will help. Lie down on the couch; let her administer to you. I must return to my couch also; the pains grow more rapid. . . ."

Francis felt the huge paw of the quill come shaggily over his face. A strange, pleasant odor enveloped him, his body grew light, weightless, as he greeted the sleep that followed. He felt his mask being removed. . . .

Quillian pads bedecked his chest plate, comforting the burning sensation in his breast. Long stepfuls of time flowed around his eyes in whorls and eddies, disfiguring the numbness between his eyebrows. His ridges felt struck by lightning, frizzled and gunked with electrostatic gibberish. He tried to speak, but the words came darkly and stuck against the mucilage of his tongue.

"Come, help me," he wanted to say. "Where is the potion, the draught of life? I thirst."

He shelled his cup of consciousness for a pea-sized glandular response. Ganglia after ganglia told him to keep his head down, to keep firing. The strain was too great, the thin wire of his tension twanged and snapped. His mind surfaced and gulped at reality.

"Are you feeling better now, Francis? You were tired and you rested long."

Francis began to focus his eyes, his mucous body responding to some primeval urge. As his eyes cleared, Rochalle's draped arms became filled with living stuff. The child!

"The child is born," gasped Francis.

"Yes, you were not on hand for the unveiling. But we all fared well indeed. The quill's performance was expert. Come, Francis, sit and hold your son."

"My son? Not a girl?"

Rochalle extended the child toward Francis who hesitated nervously.

"But what if I should drop it?"

"Hold it like this, the head . . . behind the body for support. . . ."

"I have him, I have him. How he squirms! My son, my son. What's this . . . what's this . . . what are these sounds of displeasure?"

"He hungers, Francis; he wants to feed."

"Then take him and suckle him well; he'll need to be strong. Look, his eyes, they're as big and blue as any quill cub's. . . ."

"Yes, they're beautiful. There, you see, he's quiet now. He has what he wants, just like any spoiled man. Just like his father."

"What about shots? He must have his plague inoculation. And his anemia test, what about that? And the matter of his Blood Card. So many things—"

"Don't worry, Francis, it will all be managed. Babies have been born before in far worse surroundings."

"But not for the last two thousand years, they haven't. The Baron, the Baron must know of this. We'll make him the . . . the . . . godfather!"

"Is that wise, to let him know? The Dooms proscribe against—"

"How could the Baron object? Remember, I know him well. He has changed, mellowed. The Dooms no longer are enforced. . . . Why, just the other day a quill couple were released unpunished after being apprehended in the act of intercourse. The times have changed. The Baron will be pleased. After all, it is a most historic occasion not only for us but for the entire Dominion."

"And considering that the Baron is the godfather . . ." added Rochalle.

"Yes, yes, godfather, excellent suggestion, Francis, old boy. Well put.

"Comb his hair, scrub his cheeks and in a wink I'll have returned with the Baron. Rest, my dear, rest."

"Please, Francis, don't fret so, you'll be mistaken for a schoolboy out on St. Agnes's Eve. . . ."

"Yes, I . . . St. Agnes's Eve . . . is today . . . ? But the Spore . . ."

"What is it, Francis, what's wrong?"

"Today, the Spore come forth, the pernicious little creatures shall crawl forth and—"

"And what?"

"And destroy our child and all other children that may ever be. I must find their nesting ground; I have only scant hours."

"But, Francis—"

"I must go."

Q

He passed the Piltdown Inn and the Topiary Gardens near Chelsea. He passed the fences of the Burning House Perimeter, passed the lumbering gangs of quill working the roadbeds. Little recognizance he felt, less recognition of the landscape encrusting the cliffs and gullies. He continued on his way, full blown with necrotic daydreams, the demon Spore assaulting his Rochalle. Faint stabs of sunlight fingered the highway, lighting his way through the metropolis. Hard clouds battered the skies as he climbed the stiff incline of the hill. He crested the hill and stood catching his face and breath after the steep ascent. He fleetingly glanced at the City below, obscured by the huge clouds tumbling overhead.

"Froth!" he called out loudly, cupping his hands, megaphoning his entreaty. "Froth, come forth."

Like beaten eggs, the clouds seemed to fluff up, then spill down the sky. Carrying the load of chill air behind his collar, Francis hunched with the cold. Burrowing his hands into the folds of his face, he called out, "Froth!"

Presently there was a deep rumbling and the sound of escaping gases. Soil and gravel welled up, cracked, and disintegrated to reveal the Froth. The Froth, smiling.

"Sir Francis, so good to see you so soon again. You've located the Spore, destroyed them? Yes?"

"No, but I have further questions to put to you. Rochalle, by your innuendo, was incriminated, but my investigation repudiates your accusations."

"Ah, but I made no accusations, only offered a working hypothesis."

"Perhaps then you would like to re-evaluate your logic?"

"Yes, Sir Francis, I see now that only with the Baron's full co-operation could you possibly overcome the work of the Spore Device. Go to him, enlist his aid and power. I can see you are concerned about the impending duel forming up between the quill legions and your fellow troopers."

"Yes, have you any communications?"

"Come closer, Sir Francis, gaze into my central eye. Come closer. That's better. Now, look deep into the reflection there. I think you will be able to espy the activities now in progress."

Q

Marshaling his forces, Francis overcame his initial repugnance and suspicion, stepped closer to the Froth, focused in on the central eye turret, keeping his mind from the thousand hanging threads and appendages oscillating from the form of the creature. Within the eye, the panorama of the sea and shore took shape, great contingents of floating quill lay in the wet foam and swells just beyond the breakers. Through the dense foliage the first gleaming face plates—troopers—glinted in the sunlight reflected from the water. Light waves rippled and flickered as heavy weapons were entrenched, calibrated, and primed. Against the busy flurry of the troopers, the quill flotilla seemed acquiescent, weirdly lethargic, and unperturbed. To the horizon their steaming bulks shown, yet absent was the Great Quill himself. The other quills seemed without life, floating in the waves.

"But the Quill is not there. . . ."

"He will return and that will signal the attack."

The vision faded and Francis faced the cold, glowing eyes of the Froth with apprehension once more stepping back.

"You fear for the world, Sir Francis, but, remember, there is so much more cosmic gore."

Francis did not like the laughter of the creature. It was as if it, and only it, was privy to some great jest, some obvious joke to which Francis was blind. Grimly Francis viewed the Froth's bizarre form.

"Froth, my son is born unto me today, and I would have this world saved for him. Please . . . please, help me locate the Spore breeding ground before it is too late."

"Ah, yes, my old zoological days, this all reminds me of them so vividly. A fledgling planet struggling for its existence, and then what happens? The circus comes to town and diverts the people for a moment, diverts them from irony and tragedy, gives them comedy, a stick to stand on, an oar to cast into the swirling whirlpool of disaster. Shipwrecked on this world, I notch the centuries on the trunks of long since petrified trees, my own voice becomes a stranger to me below the mantle of earth I draw over me. You come, waken me from my sleep, cast aspersions in my face, clamor for aid, demand of me miracles. But what am I or what was I? Merely a gamekeeper, a custodian of bizarre and often inimical creatures. Say by chance or fortune,

I came to know both humankind and Sporedom and now my shepherd's staff is torn from my hands and I must nurse the world back to sanity. You call forth a millstone about my neck, poet's words and desire, desire and shackle of illusion, the illusion that the center of the universe is a woman's womb, and the music of the sphere but a baby's cry. Mere mortals they call, but you would bedevil the gods with your entreaties for the eternal now. Greedy carnivores, wholesale omnivores. You, tidy little creature before, metal plated and dreamily secure, why would I want to take any more part in all this but that of a bystander, an innocent onlooker? Marvel of it all, you bless and curse in one breath your world. You and your whirligig paradox. But truly I love you for it."

"Then you will help?"

"All my discourse has not been for naught but that very aim. To help you, to help lift ye the veils from your eyes. The Spore. That great immortal danger, that stalking predator of man, he lurks, he lurks."

"Where, where is its lair?"

"It is one of many. He knows."

"Who knows? The Quill? The Baron? Lombard? You, Froth?"

"Yes. Surely one of them. Seek one and you shall find them all; seek them all and you shall find the one."

"Then it is the Baron?"

"He quotes poetry, does he not?"

"Poetry? Lombard quotes poetry—then Lombard, he is the source."

"Does he control the seas?"

"The Quill floats through the seas. It is he?"

"Sir Francis, animal acts found a diminishing return of enthusiasm since I began my travels, eons ago. I would like to enter some new endeavor, perhaps purchase a small asteroid somewhere and raise magnetic storms."

"You jest with me, Froth."

"Of course I jest with you, Sir Francis."

"Tread lightly; I will not take the passing of the world lightly.

And don't proffer me up some absurd excuses of cosmic gore, so much gore, I've had enough."

"Yes, I can see that. Well, then, perhaps you should set sail for the front lines where the combatants face off for the final conflict to make the world safe for the quill, or the Dominion, or whosoever shall win the momentary victory. Until the Spore take control . . . You'll find your answers in the heat of battle, Sir Francis. Hurry now, I think I hear that first shot. . . ."

Q

Reverberations of lost summers' squeals turned sausage links in the air over Francis' head. The gunship's propeller blades sliced the thick air into wettish smog. Hoarsely, Francis ordered the craft toward the crags and tortured rocks of the island just to the east of the battleground, the larger of the Orkney Islands.

The volcanic pumice bit into his boot, scratched the leather, and made walking difficult. The light was poor at noon, heavy mists floated listlessly in the stagnant air; the splash of the waves against the shore added to the grayness. Francis climbed to the higher ground and was allowed entrance into the makeshift battle station. Troopers sat about on the sharp stones, numbly remembering the first brief skirmish. Already some felt the mortality of their quickly festering wounds. A moan, a curse, the hiss of the wind through the rocks colored the outcome of the fight.

Francis found the Baron deeply enmeshed in a relief map on a table surrounded by his battle-bruised lieutenants. They turned when Francis entered.

Without a word they turned back to their consultation with the map. Francis could hear their muffled voices behind their war masks, watched as their hands grappled with the outcome of the previous encounter with the behemoth sea quills. Toy ships and men were broken and scattered, black and red and black again, amid the scrambled remains of vehicles and land masses too heavy with dead blood to displace much more than an analytical response from the veteran tacticians.

"More firepower on this perimeter. . . . No, the reserve battalion should have been moved in under the barrage. The quill knew our efforts were in vain, they had our every move. . . . A traitor, a spy? Within our own ranks. But who? Who but us could have known, we were all joined in battle. . . ."

They turned when the Baron's massive metal armor pivoted toward Francis, warming his gloves at the fire in the wall grating. He felt their metal-rimmed eyes heavy upon the nape of his neck. He faced their steely stares.

"Sir Francis, where were you when the hostilities broke out?" said the battalion commander.

"Hostilities?"

"The fire fight with the quill, last night. We were cut to ribbons."

"Eaten alive," the infantry colonel added.

"Crushed," murmured the artillery expert.

"Last night I spent in transit from the Citadel here. I was in the air, I suppose, during the conflict. Our troops did not fare well, it seems, but perhaps I am not too late to forestall further carnage. We waste our men and munitions on the wrong enemy; the quill are not our foe. The Spore. They are our mortal foe. Let us be gone from this war field. The sea runs red with wasted blood. Call our guns away, retrace our bullets. Roll back the fleet."

"You call for retreat, for surrender, Sir Francis?" asked the commander.

"We will never capitulate to those loathsome creatures, their jaws grisly grinning with the corpses of our comrades," cursed the colonel.

"Yes, our comrades' gore floats on the water and you cry for panic, for defeat," said the commander, pounding the table.

"Gore? So much more gore is there, wordfuls of gore. Do not persecute Sir Francis so," spoke the Baron quietly.

"I dare call his words treason," called out the battalion commander.

"Now, gentlemen, in the heat of the moment and the grief of the hour, we are too quick to judgment. Sir Francis would not betray his fellows in the gape of death. Would you, Sir Francis?" said the Baron.

"I will not honor their accusations with an answer. I came here hoping to speak reason with you."

"Please forgive us, Sir Francis," said the Baron.

Everyone looked at each other in mild amazement at the Baron's apology.

"Come, sit with us, give us of your wisdom and insight into the morrow's battle plan. Here we sketch the defeat of the creatures and send them to the slime below. Here, take this chair," said the Baron.

Francis slowly sat himself at the table, belligerent toward the battle-grimed faces of the soldiers.

"What can you offer us in strategy and tact, Sir Francis, for we will not give up the field of battle. Resign yourself to the task assigned, plot the course. We will listen to your experience and valor's rightful credit. Forbear with us for our hot tempers and all too ready vituperations. Please, Sir Francis, join your brothers-in-arms at this moment of grave danger."

The ring of helmeted men waited for Francis' response. He knew these men well, had fought with them, some of them from the old school and the street-fighting days. And the troopers waiting outside and in bivouac, they too, had been under his command. He owed them much for their personal sacrifice and courage, albeit misguided and maldirected. He could not let them die, even though they had chosen the way themselves. They were ignorant men, yet men of honor and loyalty.

"The fools," he muttered, then moved his chair into the center of the conference table.

Q

"Sir Francis, this is the present situation. Whether due to blunder, fate, or fortune, we occupy this small island while all around us, hidden by the mists, the quill lay in wait. They sneak up to the shore and drag any unwary trooper into the deep water. The mists and fog make it impossible to evacuate our men even if we could safely bring any gunships in. At the outset the quill divided our forces from each other, many of the rafts were lost or strayed away into the fog. We still have no accurate count of our casualties or our surviving troopers."

"And this is our position, the crest of the southern hill?" asked Francis, pointing at the map.

"Yes," said the commander.

"What is the displacement of the troopers?"

"They lie straggled all about the island, in general disarray; many of the wounded are quartered near our command post. Also, a disciplined force of the Burning House Troopers are still intact and await our orders. They fared well in the initial onslaught."

Francis looked toward the Baron who had not spoken while his commanders relayed the dismal information. Many bullet scratches scarred the Baron's battle armor, heavy dents marked many a quill blow.

"The firing was intense; some of our troopers were rattled, fired into the fog and struck down many of their own; even the Baron was caught in the withering crossfire effected, ironically by our own men," said the colonel.

"Again, the immortal Baron, though battered, stood well up behind his invulnerability," said the gunship commander.

"Yes, the Baron walked among the panicky men, amidst the shelling and calmed them, ended the erratic firing, regrouped what units were still recognizable," said the colonel.

"Where are the quill now?"

"They are all around us, encircle us, but the bulk of their forces lie to the south. Our sensors detect the heaviest register in that area, more pounds of quill flesh per cubic yard."

"But the quill have not taken any of the island itself?" pondered Francis.

"No, our firepower has kept them from all but the shoals and fringes of the island."

"I see. And what heavy weapons do we have?"

"A few light fire tongs, two field blowsers, and one command car."

"Any fire roaches?" asked Francis.

"Fire roaches?"

"Yes, the Burning House Troopers carry them as standard issue," said Francis.

"I can check that," said the colonel.

"Collect them all and put them in the command vehicle. Call up all the forces from the shore areas and have them congregate on this hill," said Francis with finality.

"But, Sir Francis, that will leave the island undefended, an easy mark for the quill to overrun," said the commander.

"Will you gather the fire roaches, Colonel?"

"Do as Sir Francis asks," said the Baron quietly.

"Yes, sir," said the colonel who saluted, turned, and went in search of weapons.

Q

Froth counted the stars. Heavy with the accustomed frost, he made the number sing to him, call him into the folds of the space. He sighed and tore the wall of earth from round his waist and wrested the boulders from his chest.

He surveyed the countryside and airways for sight of moving objects. No objects appeared and he went about his task. Yearly the sprouts about his buried body had to be replanted, tilled, and slightly aged. Tooling about the soil, mucking the fertilizer beneath the soft-bellied shoots, he could sense their germinal life, twitching beneath his hand hook.

The sky was abnormally clear, portentous, he thought, of things to come. He hurried about, rearranging the soil, the rubble, and stones into a fit chaos. Tucking in the loose leaves he made a nest of sorts and waited. His song would attract notice soon. Was that not a flight of brain bags on the horizon? Yes, it was. And *she* must be there obscured by the thick forest. The brain bags heralded her approach.

It was not the traditional nesting grounds, but it would make do. She would not mind, he knew.

It had been so long, so very long since he had mated. Could

he remember the song? He laughed to himself. He called out again. There was a long silence, and then, the faintest sound of a reply from the distance, beyond the maroon hills. Was it an echo or her call in response? So faint was the sound, he could not tell. But then it came again and again to his straining ear sacs. Yes, it was a she.

She came so quickly through the brush that a screen of dust rose. Heartily he called out, soof-soofing; greatly anticipating her arrival he felt strengths stirring, pulses rising. "Soof, soof," he sang. Ringing back the chimelike sounds, a fainter, "soof, soof." The call drew closer, Froth's spine quivered, tingled. He leapt in the nest and waited, his ductless glands opening and closing, gushing out. Gush. A full leap and she was on him, springing from the underbrush into the mad tangle of his writhing limbs; then they were upon each other, singing and gushing, gushing and singing. The nest was a flurring of bodies, momentous titanic thrashings, shaking the ground. Their song joined for that second of utter harmony, the ecstasy shimmering up into the sky in which their mammoth bodies floated.

Wind-swept, the leaves tumbled about their motionless forms; honeydew settled among their body cavities. He caressed the fur on her flanks; she sang a soft melody under his arm. Froth, fulfilled, looked deeply into the fathomless eyes of the she-creature, loving her every drop. She clambered among his fondest memories, others faded beside her. From out of all time and space, this she had come to him, answering the ancient mating call, yet he could not but feel that chance had little to do with it, that destiny, perhaps past lives, had brought them together for their vast love-making and spawning.

The ground settled its last tremblings beneath their half sleep, assuaging them into resplendent dozing. The plummage on his body, more lustrous and fulsome after the encounter, lay protectively over her nubile form, her body beautiful. Clinging to her unknown lover, she grew the spawn within her center, as the sun began setting over them. Bronze light played upon the upturning of her abdomen as the swift birthing began to culminate. A new one had been made—to oversee the New Era.

Q

In the far-distant waters, the sea quill became aware of the happenings on that hillock far away. Their voices trumpeted their praise, their flippers beat the sea to frothful congratulations. Booming upward their massed call shook the small island and Francis thereupon. The momentous birth passed unnoticed to the band of armed men, intent on the killing at hand. They fancied they heard dull explosions from the rim of the island, paying small heed to the nagging intuition in the forepoints of their brains. Something was happening, something planing up from the depths of the galaxy, from the hub of the wheel within the hubs of the ever-recurring wheels.

Steering the command car away from the mud clogging the tire chains, Francis cradled his weapon across his neck and slid in behind the controls. Heavy hatches sealed, he turned the ignition. The opposite door opened and the Baron came aboard. They stared at one another, unspeaking, merged at last, within the common goal, strung to the same instrument of their common fate, they took their eyes to the path leading down into the beach and the massed landing of the quill legions. The sun had just fallen into darkness.

Bursts of rocket and small-arms fire pocked the air over them and tore hunks from the rock as they sped at the sharp angle of descent. Some quill scouts were chanced upon by the bright light of the search lamp, soon followed by the sear of tracer shells from the Baron's fire tong. They fell and smoldered. Quickly brain bags fastened upon their corpses. The command car gained speed as it careened down the hill; heavy thuds fell around as quill after desperate quill threw themselves against the vehicle as if they sensed what lay in store.

Francis looked once more at the Baron whose massive arms cradled the satchels of fire roaches, their fuses set and primed. He nodded. Francis bore down on the accelerator, slicing through the cordons of quill, their bodies hurtling through the air to land on the damp sand. The command car churning deeply into their midsts, targeting for the center and the Great Quill himself, who stood out like a banner, huge and fearsome.

The charges would explode upon contact with his monstrous body. And then they were upon him, Francis stood the wheel straight into the Quill whose jaws opened ready to devour just as the Baron tossed the satchels into the air. The charges and the Quill's jaws met in mid-air. Francis drove the vehicle into his knees and knew no more.

Q

The battle had come, his child had been born, the Quill had been killed, the Spore lay in ambush somewhere. Frogs and leopards, puma-spotted sea quill bodies hung over the rocks and fender skirts, draped in death. Bloody mouthed and sand encrusted, Francis felt his face come up out of the shallow surf, his eyes heavy with brine and pain. Scenes from the past fought hand to hand with the present nightmare, throats were cut, arms seared to ground meat. The anguished cries of the dead and dying littered the fog; broken screams fell among the crest and valleys of the waves washing the beach clear of the dead and drowning the maimed.

His mind was still reeling with images of the Baron, the Quill, and the Froth, all three chorusing the refrain of "the world, the world, so many more, come we plunder through cosmic gore." Their metallic voices harmonized sickeningly until by sheer force of will Francis forced them from his delirium. But something of the vision remained with him.

Hung over the wrecked hulk of the command vehicle lay the body of the Baron. It did not move. Francis, on hands and knees, waited a long time in the sand and water for the Baron to move, to rise up, to tower over the beach, but the mirrored body did not. No arm fluttered beside the plume of his headgear; no arm or leg; the heavy vizor neither cleaved now nor did the fire tong spit fiery death. The Baron's body was without life; it appeared like the vacated shell of a crab, and Francis scuttled over to it, too weak and dizzy to stand.

He touched the heavy gauntlet of the massive arm. There was no response. He thought of putting the body down onto the soft sand, from off the jagged metal of the wreck, but he knew it would take a wrecking crew and chains to move the incredible weight. Probably a raft to float it along the current, home. But the painful lacerated edges of the metal digging into the Baron's side caused Francis to throw his weight against the mountain of metal in a desperate effort to move it, although futility sounded in his grunt.

To his amazement the body not only moved, it floated easily off into the light breeze, not with the weight of granite but of balsa wood. Francis went to the other side of the debris where the body had drifted to rest, its arms and legs crumbled absurdly rubberlike. "Can death be so comfortable?" wondered Francis aloud to the corpses strewn about him.

Francis poked the massive chest plate with a smoke-blackened finger, a light jab. The body skittered across the sand as if helium filled its innards. Francis could not believe. He watched the body tumble across the beach until it stopped, lodged against more blackened rubble. Francis came closer, the rubble became the burnt and splintered bulk of the Quill, its jaws bent askew by the blast, its stomach gaping a huge tear from the explosive it had attempted to swallow.

The two bodies hugged each other, fraternal in their common disaster. As Francis kneeled by their lifeless shells, Dominion troopers and quill legionnaires slowly gathered about, weaponless, with the heat of battle dragging at their eyelids. Before them lay their symbols, their truth; their leaders, grappling each other, forever comrades. The beach heard only the low hum of the breeze, the slight crunch of sand underfoot as the soldiers huddled together, paying tribute to their fallen commanders.

Francis began to dig a hole in the soft moist sand, with his hands. Soon others joined him, digging together, side by side. The hole deepened into a pit and widened into a trench as the moon began to fall beneath the blue-black waves. The bodies were gently lowered into the common grave and the sand refilled by hand, each warrior pushing the sand over the sleeping faces.

Q

When the grave was filled, the combatants trudged off, barely looking at one another. Francis watched the beaches clear as the gunship crews picked up the survivors. Soon the sound of their departure melded with the strokes of the quills paddling away from the island. The disconsolate pile of coral rock marking the grave already struggled to fend off the encroaching sweep of the sand. Soon all traces would be gone of it, thought Francis, perhaps even the island would sink beneath the thirsty waves as had the others. As Francis walked away to the gunship hovering in wait for him, the last of the moon's rays sparkled against the brain bags settling over the beach.

Q

Francis did not go directly to his room nor did he pass the prison walls of the Burning House; he stood within its ominous shadow strung with wire and barbs, the odyssey of his life passing before him in the pale glow of dawn.

The death of the Baron and, in a profound yet mute way, also the death of the Great Quill left him empty; his body began to feel devoid of substance, a hollow container for his depression. He shuffled along in the white gravel and manicured plastic shrubbery, hands clasped behind his long leather coat. The lapels faltered and flapped in the swirls of wind that hurried around the corners of the labyrinth walls. A frost had risen and he could smell the smudge pots' sticky heat. It was St. Agnes's Eve. The old people would be gathered about, listening to the oldest read poetry or sing some ancient song. Strains of "Good King Wenceslaus" eddied through his ears, reddened from the cold. There was nothing he could do, nothing. It had all come to pass. The Baron had died, the duomillennia had ended, the Spore was once more unleashed, the Sisyphean agonies again set into motion. What madness more to come? The Froth and his sly dream to gain ownership of the planet, desert though it may become after the Spore had lapped up the moisture from the veins and capillaries of the world. Still that seemed strange to him, the Spore literally drinking the world dry, tipsy with ocean-filled bellies. Literal, yes, perhaps too literal, was his interpretation of the Froth's often esoteric wordings. The Spore spawning forth from the earth from some secret nesting place . . . Why should he believe what this alien said?

Words began to collide and echo from each other . . . nest . . . spawn . . . cosmic gore . . . That nebulous fog in the back of his brain began to clear. Incredible realizations began to take shape. He hurried to Rochalle's chamber and the child.

The guards stood apart for him, seemed to snap almost too readily to their attention, lapsed into peripheral awareness as Francis entered the suite. Rochalle, her long tresses turned to pure light by the lamp fixture overhead, looked up from the feeding lips of her young son, smiling at Francis.

"How is the child, Rochalle?"

"He has no bottom to his stomach, he eats so. He could drink the oceans dry, I think, if he were so inclined. But the taste is too bitter."

Francis stood with her small joke trembling his hands.

"Are you trying to tell me something, Rochalle?"

She looked at him, a different expression forming her face. Even through her feeding mask, he could see the change. She nodded, yes.

"Is this, my child, the Spawn of the Spore?" His voice shook.

"Yes," she answered. "And the Spawn of Quill. And the Spawn of Froth."

Francis stared at the child's white head, thin blue veins shone beneath the translucent skin. Yet it did not seem alien to him as it suckled its mother's breast. But it was Spore and it was human.

"I think I must kill it," he said without emotion.

Rochalle looked up into his eyes, the infant cradled within her arms. Francis expected some reply from her, some protestation, but none came. Only the baby's gurgling sounds ceased as it let go the nipple and turned its face toward Francis. The eyes of the child, blue and saucerlike, held Francis in fascination as if they spoke to him. "No, you need not kill me," came the voice from the small red lips.

Francis' head jerked back. The baby had spoken, had spoken. Francis shook his head. "No, this cannot be. I am run amuck. I hear the child speak."

"It is all right, Francis," said Rochalle, drying the baby's lips with adoration. "You should know that all is well. The Spore is born."

"The Spore is born? My God, what is this madness!"

"The Spore is born. Simply that."

"But the Spore, they are—"

"Our enemies?"

"Yes, they seek to destroy us."

"Us? But who, who are those you call us, Francis?"

"You, me, the child. . . ."

"Spore. We are all Spore, have always been Spore."

"But the Froth, the Baron, even the Great Quill, they all spoke of the Spore always as enemies, destroyers."

"But who are these you speak of, this Froth, the Quill, even the Baron himself?"

"The Baron is dead, Rochalle; he died by my side as he and I killed the Great Quill."

"Killed the Great Quill?"

"Why do you laugh? Share the jest with me."

"The Quill cannot be destroyed, not any more than could the Baron."

"I buried both with my own hands. I threw the sand over their burnt-out faces."

"Prepare yourself, Francis; pull back those drapes."

With the sash cord in his hand, Francis drew back the heavy drapery. There stood the Baron.

The Baron stood, gleaming, polished brighter than Francis had ever seen, polished so brightly that it could only be . . .

"This is not the Baron, merely his armor, brand-new armor plating. No one lives inside."

"True, Francis, true. And always true."

"If this is the Baron, then where is the Great Quill? Do you have his carcass dried out and mounted?"

"This is no taxidermy," she said, as the Great Quill slowly slid around the corner, his huge forehead nearly grazing the ceiling. His massive bulk, fur-shagged and ponderous, heaved gently to Rochalle's side.

"Did you not remember that I can reconstitute my body at will, Sir Francis? This is merely one of many you see before you."

"And in more ways than one, my friend."

The new voice was that of Froth, foreshortened to a moderate size, who entered through the archway.

There before Francis' eyes, standing side by side, the three formidable beings stood in array. The Baron's seven-foot mirrored armor; the Quill and his gaping jaws and huge fathomless eyes; and the Froth, feathered and iridescent.

"I am not the fool asleep under the hill, Sir Francis. But I am the keeper of the game and not the animals from the zoo, lost eons ago, but The Game, the game we play. May I introduce the principal players?

"The Baron. The figure of authority, the warrior, the titan, the very Citadel of physical existence himself. And yet, a metal mirror, a polished mirror, is he. Later you will have to look into that mirror again, Sir Francis. But first, let me continue, let me give ample credit to those players upon the field. The second character, the Great Quill, revolutionary saint, god incarnate, garbage eater, the great contradiction, the Paradox. All very well done. Fomented a revolution, too. But you can see there is little difference between the Quill and the Baron, gemini more or less, twins, opposite sides of the coin, and all that."

"And the Spore, where are they?"

"Why, Rochalle told you that. She and her son are Spore, you are Spore, the whole world's Spore; remember so much cosmic gore. I thought surely the repetition of those words by the Baron, then the Quill, and myself, might move you to question."

"And they did, indeed. So what you are telling me is that there is no enemy, no Spore, that we are the Spore. But I take it all this is about to pass, the age is ending, a new one coming."

"More or less. But after all, Francis, you were an assassin, the High Executioner. Something will have to be paid for that."

"Paid to who?" said Francis, stiffening.

"Paid to me," said Froth.

"And who are you, Gamekeeper?"

"In one of my aspects you knew me as the Adjudicator, the Cleanser of Zeroes—"

"Lombard!"

"Yes. Please put your weapon down, Sir Francis, the project is already completed. You have a new role to play in the New Era."

"I would die before becoming your pawn."

"Dying, let's not talk of such things on a beautiful day such as it is. You are not under my control. We are all within the grip of the cosmic laugh, Infinity's mirth. Enjoy it. Enjoy your child."

"Yes, Father, enjoy me. I come but once every two thousand years."

"So did the Quill. . . ."

"So did Froth. . . ."

"So did the Baron. . . ."

They all spoke in unison, the Baron, Froth, the Quill, Rochalle and the Baby. . . .

Froth spoke after a silence.

"Sir Francis, it is time you looked into the mirror, saw your face of flesh."

He was drawn over to the Baron's body by the hands all around him. They took away his mask.

"Look deeply into the shine, Sir Francis. What do you see? What do you see?"

Francis looked into the polished metal towering above him. He could not take his eyes from it, he felt himself being drawn into the reflection, into the hollow shell before him.

"It's your turn now, Sir Francis, your turn to be the Baron."

Inside the seven-foot metal body, Francis, no longer Francis as that consciousness slipped away, cried out, "But who are you, if not I, and I you?!!"

A cheer rose up, the sound rolling as an ocean, as those about him clapped in applause.

"Yes," said the blue-eyed baby in Rochalle's arms. "Yes, Father, you are exactly right."